Razzle

Also by Ellen Wittlinger

Gracie's Girl

What's in a Name

Hard Love

The Long Night of Leo and Bree

Razzle

Ellen Wittlinger

Simon Pulse

New York London Toronto Sydney Singapore

First Simon Pulse edition March 2003

Copyright © 2001 by Ellen Wittlinger

SIMON PULSE
An imprint of Simon & Schuster
Children's Publishing Division
1230 Avenue of the Americas
New York, NY 10020

Also available in a Simon & Schuster Books for Young Readers hardcover edition.
The text of this book was set in Bembo.

Printed in the United States of America
6 8 10 9 7 5

The Library of Congress has cataloged the hardcover edition as follows:
Wittlinger, Ellen.
Razzle / Ellen Wittlinger—1st ed.
p. cm.
Summary: When his retired parents buy a group of tourist cabins on Cape Cod, fifteen-year-old Kenyon Baker's days are filled with repair work until he becomes friends with an eccentric girl and makes her the subject of a series of photographs.
ISBN 0-689-83565-5 (hc.)
[1. Family Life—Fiction. 2. Photography—Fiction. 3. Friendship—Fiction.]
I. Title
PZ7.W78436 Raz 2001
[Fic] dc—21
00067975
ISBN 0-689-85600-8 (Simon Pulse pbk.)

For Kate and Morgan
and for anyone who's ever had sand in their shoes

With grateful thanks to my editor, David Gale, his
assistants, John Rudolph and Elena Murphy, and my agent,
Ginger Knowlton; and to Pat Lowery Collins, Suzanne
Freeman, and Anita Riggio for their help and advice on
the manuscript

Special thanks also to the Fine Arts Work Center in
Provincetown, Massachusetts

Razzle

one

Looking back, I'd have to say my life was one long snooze until the day I met Razzle Penney at the Truro dump. Mom had forced me to go with her that morning. She rationalized my servitude by telling me lifting junk would bulk up the muscles in my scrawny arms. Like I cared.

But there I was at the dump at ten o'clock lugging garbage out of the station wagon, then heaving it over the railing into the big container that would truck it off into oblivion. Make it disappear. So people didn't have to look at piles of discarded crap and think about how quickly their new piece of plastic from Wal-Mart or that cute little Gap outfit had turned into trash.

Okay, I was in a cynical mood that morning. It was the mood I'd been in for two weeks, ever since we'd relocated to that skinny little town with the unpronounceable name way out near the end of the sandy finger of vacationland called Cape Cod. We'd moved here from Boston, where I'd grown up in blessed invisibility in the shadow of the Hancock Tower and the Prudential Center, protected on all sides by insurance.

And now I was being turned into a sanitation engineer because the cottage colony my parents had just purchased

came with enough broken-down furniture to redecorate
Transylvania. Mom intended to refurbish the places in "a
simple style that emphasizes the view." I guess that subscrip-
tion to *Travel & Leisure* magazine wasn't wasted on her
because the view is absolutely the *only* aspect of these cottages that would make anybody in their right mind vacation
here.

The little houses are lined up right along a main road, so
the bedrooms are always lit up by headlights from cars that
seem to be driving right through the living rooms. Of
course, on the other side they open up on to the beach, the
whole line of them, right on the curve of Cape Cod Bay
where you can watch the sun rise over Wellfleet and set over
Provincetown. Which even *I* enjoyed the one time we came
here as tourists and weren't responsible for anything but getting tan.

Owning the place was a different story altogether. The old
mattresses, squeaky bed frames, and plywood bureaus with
drawers that stuck like they'd been glued shut had been
hauled away last week by an odd-jobs guy with a big truck.
What was left for us to bag and discard were mostly the "dec-
orative" items, the seagull paintings and filthy curtains, and
various guest leftovers: moldy sheets, moldy towels, moldy
swimming suits, moldy condoms. It was not the first time I'd
thought about how the guy who sold us these rattraps must
be laughing his ass off over the city slickers who'd bought
thirteen rotted-out shacks with bad plumbing.

Once we'd gotten rid of our junk, I looked around at the
dump. I had to admit, the one thing this town had going for
it was great photographic opportunities. Everywhere I
looked there were weird vistas and odd juxtapositions, and

the dump was no different. I hadn't brought my camera, but I took it all in anyway, the giant stuffed cat guarding the door of a recycling shed while a small pink pony trotted across the top door frame; aluminum cans crushed together into two-foot squares and stacked like Andy Warhol's idea of stairs; and a crooked little shack that looked like an outhouse without a door and had KEEP OUT written across the side in red paint.

An elderly woman wearing a raincoat, pink hair rollers, and fuzzy slippers that looked like small spotted cows got out of an ancient Dodge to toss three or four plastic ginger ale bottles into a container that read: REFUNDABLE BOTTLES AND CANS—A FRIENDS OF THE TRURO COUNCIL ON AGING PROJECT. How could she be in such a hurry to contribute her four bottles that she'd go out in public looking like that?

How could I be a mere two and a half hours from Boston? Everything, every*body* seemed different. The sun was brighter. The wind was stronger. And the people I'd seen so far seemed . . . bigger. Not in size, but in personality or something. They all seemed to stick out in ways I never noticed people sticking out in the city. Maybe it didn't have as much to do with cow slippers as with the fact that there weren't as many of them, so they spread out more, took up as much space as they wanted to.

I should have known better than to go out without my camera, but I think I was half afraid Mom would pitch it into a Dumpster too in her frenzy to unload everything in sight. She'd already gotten back in the car when I noticed the girl walking toward us. She was as tall as me but even skinnier, and even though she was walking fast, her long arms and legs seemed to sort of swirl around her in this lazy way, like all the joints weren't connected up quite right. Her buzz cut hairdo and the black short shorts and tank top added to the vision of a leggy bug or a jellyfish swimming over to us.

"Let's go, Kenny. I've got lots more to do today," Mom said.

"I think somebody wants to talk to us," I said.

"Who?"

By that time the girl had gotten close enough to yell. "Did I see you guys pitch a lamp in the Dumpster?"

Mom leaned out the window. "Yes, we did. Is there a problem?"

"Whyn't you bring it to the Swap Shop? Somebody mighta used it." I was glad her glare was directed toward Mom.

"The what?"

The girl pointed in back of her to a low, gray-shingled structure with a wheelchair ramp leading inside. "The Swap Shop. You should bring your good stuff in there. Then people who need things can get 'em free."

Mom laughed. "Oh, honey, that old lamp didn't even work."

Our interrogator was not impressed. "So? Anybody can fix a goddamn lamp."

As soon as she hears a swear word Mom switches into schoolteacher mode—it's an easy transformation—she taught ninth-grade Spanish for twenty-four years. (I took French.) No more "honey" for our new friend now.

"I don't think it's really any of your business what we do with our old furniture!"

"It's my *job*," she said. She sounded kind of surprised that we didn't already know this. "I run the Swap Shop. People come in all the time looking for lamps. And then you throw one away, just like that!" She whipped one long arm up in the air as if heaving an unwanted object casually over her shoulder.

"Is it your job to harass people?" my mother said.

She shook her head. "I'm not harassing you. I'm just telling you."

"Well, thank you for the information." I knew Mom was pissed; she looked over at me still standing outside the car, admiring the lip this kid was giving her. "May we go now, please?"

"Have you even been inside the Swap Shop?" the girl asked me. It made me nervous that she was addressing me now. She stuck her hands on her hips where they formed perfect triangles with her curveless body.

"Me? No. We just moved here. We didn't know about it." What I was really saying was: *Don't shoot! I'm innocent!*

But she nodded. "I'll show ya then." Her wave turned into a crawl stroke as she turned and walked toward the gray building. "Come on."

What else could I do but follow? Besides, the place was just strange enough to appeal to my photographer's eye. And so was she. It would be great to get a shot of her swimming along past the recycling shed—from down low so the shed would loom above her as her thin arms floated out at her sides.

"Ken, where are you going?" Mom yelled after me. This is how being such a good kid all the time turns against you; your parents start to think you'll never do anything without their written permission.

"I just want to see the place. One minute." She'd be ready to roast my butt by the time I got back, but what the hell? All I'd been doing for two weeks was working on those stinking cottages—like I was a partner in their stupid idea or something. Most high school kids spent their summers taking trips, or going to camp, or at least getting *paid* for working. I was lucky if I got a lunch break. And this girl was the first person under thirty I'd laid eyes on since we got here.

"This is where people drop off stuff they don't want," she said as we came into an entry hall. There was a table along one wall with several grocery bags full of clothing on it and some rusty fireplace tongs. A huge bulletin board hung over the table with tacked-up appeals for lost pets, notices for tai chi classes and art openings, offers to sell fishing rods and Chihuahua puppies, and lots of apartment-wanted signs with tear-off phone number strips hanging from the bottom like fringe.

I was reading a paper that said WILL SWAP COUCH FOR TV, trying to figure out which item the writer already had and which one he wanted, when an old guy with a white beard came shoving in the door past me, grabbed the fireplace tongs, and whooped.

"Just what I wanted! Who brought these in anyway?"

"Hi, Eddie. I don't know—somebody left them by the door overnight."

"Perfect, just perfect. Any other iron come in today?"

"Not today. Just that old bedstead and you didn't want that."

"No, no. It's not junk yet. Somebody could use it." He turned to go. "Okay then. See you tomorrow, Razzle."

"Bye, Eddie." She beckoned me into the main room. "I've got it all organized in here. See? Things used to be stacked anywhere, but now it's all got a place."

"How come he wants iron stuff?" I asked her.

"Eddie's a sculptor. He welds old iron pieces into statues." She started pointing things out again. "So, I sort the clothes into these bins, the shoes go on that rack over there, books along the back wall . . ."

But I wasn't really paying attention to the tour. People out here were *so* peculiar. "Did he call you Razzle? Is that your name?"

"That's it."

"I've never heard that name before."

She shrugged. "My mother was into angels. Still is, I guess. Raziel is the Angel of Mysteries. But she thought nobody would be able to spell it or pronounce it right, so she just called me Razzle. My brother Ezra is named for the Angel of Writers. That's what my mom wanted to be, back in the day. Before she was just a screwup."

She turned back to the job at hand. "I put all the breakable kitchen stuff, like dishes and glasses and blenders, high up on the back wall. The electronics, toasters and coffeemakers and stuff, are on the low shelves—I figure kids can't break that stuff any more than it's already broken. And the toys are all together in that little enclosed space."

Razzle paused and looked squarely into my eyes. I wasn't sure what she expected me to do—praise her for her organizational skills? The place just looked like a roomful of junk to me.

"So," she said, "do you like it?"

I shrugged. "Sure. I guess it's a good job, huh?"

"It's a *great* job. And now they even pay me for it."

"They didn't always?"

"I started doing it last year because I liked seeing all the stuff that came in. Then I started fixing the place up because

I like things to be organized. So pretty soon the selectmen voted on it, and now they pay me."

I figured Mom was probably laying eggs out in the car by now. I made a slight movement toward the door. "Well, I better . . ."

"What's your name? You didn't say."

"I'm Kenyon. Kenyon Baker."

"Razzle Penney," she said, sticking out her long, thin arm so that her bony hand could grab mine and pump it up and down. She smiled, too, a lopsided, tomboyish kind of smile that made me think of a girl I used to play with in kindergarten. I liked that kid; we made monster drawings together. Kaitlin hadn't turned out to be a neatnik junkmeister, though; last time I saw her she was smoking dope behind the school with some other losers.

"You here for the summer?" she asked.

"I wish. We've moved here. Bought a cottage colony on the bay."

"Oh, you must be the ones who bought the Landmark Cottages on 6A! Right? God, I didn't think he'd ever sell those places."

"He finally found some suckers."

"They'll be fine once you fix 'em up."

"I don't know . . ."

"Sure! You got a 180 view and sand outside the back door. People will come even if the toilets *do* back up."

"How'd you know . . . ?"

But right about then my mother charged in the door; she'd obviously spent a little too much time in a hot car parked between two garbage barges. "Ken! What are you doing? I told you I need to get back!"

"Sorry. I was talking to Razzle."

"*Who?*"

"Razzle. This is Razzle."

"Oh." Mom glared at her, then leaped back and brushed at her arm. "Ooh, a spider! It was right on my shirt! Where'd it go? I *hate* spiders!" She kept brushing at herself and looking around.

"This place is full of spiders, but most of them are harmless," Razzle said. "The average person swallows eight spiders in their lifetime. Usually at night. Without even realizing it."

"Thank you. There's a fact I would rather not have known," Mom said, shivering. You could tell the spider incident had gotten on her last nerve. "Ken, you can talk to"— she waved her hand in Razzle's direction—"this girl some other time."

"Razzle," she said to refresh Mom's memory. "I'm here nine to three, Monday through Thursday, and sometimes Saturday mornings, unless I'm at the flea with Billie."

"Okay I'll come back," I said.

"Come tomorrow," she ordered. "Thursdays are always good."

"I'll try." She made me laugh, but I have to confess, I wasn't quite sure if I was laughing *with* her or *at* her.

"Bye, Kenyon," she yelled after me. "I like your name!"

"She's funny, isn't she?" I said as we climbed back into the car.

"*Funny?*" Mom tromped on the gas pedal, and we wheeled out onto the highway.

"She's downright strange. Much too outspoken for a young girl. Says whatever comes to her mind. I don't know why you told her you'd come back. She's very . . . *odd.*"

I didn't argue. The truth was, if Razzle hadn't been odd she wouldn't have *asked* me to come back. If Mom had been paying attention the last few years, she'd know that. But I guess she got tired of paying attention to teenagers after years of arguing with my sisters and then dealing with all those high school Spanish students, too.

And, of course, she didn't exactly ask for a third child. I was, as she put it, a *surprise.* Which sounded kind of nice until the time Dad threw her a surprise birthday party, and she walked in the door crying because she'd just hit a squirrel with the car, and thirty people jumped out from behind the furniture to scream at her. After everybody left she kept saying, "Don't you ever do this to me again, Ted. I *hate* surprises!"

"She's so tall and skinny," Mom said, still ruminating on Razzle as we turned onto our road.

"So am I," I reminded her.

She glanced over at me, as if she'd forgotten that. "Well, yes, but you're a boy," she said, as though one gender made a more acceptable skeleton than the other. Or, more likely, she just wasn't cutting any slack for a girl who could fix a god-damn lamp.

two

Our "colony" wasn't called Landmark Cottages anymore. Oh, no. Two retired schoolteachers like Ted and Mary Pat Baker knew they could come up with something more educational than that. So now we live in Baker's Birdhouses, each shanty soon to have its own bird name—only local birds need apply—stenciled over the door: Heron, Sandpiper, Egret, Eagle, Hawk, Plover, Cormorant, Shearwater, Loon (a very popular cabin, we would soon learn, often rented by birdbrains), Osprey, Tern, Finch, and Mockingbird. (No Gulls or Pigeons for Ted and Mary Pat.)

Mockingbird probably would have been a popular cabin too, except that it was not for rent. In the deal I'd finally struck with my parents, it had become mine for the summer. There was a price to pay, of course, but, at the time we agreed on it, no price seemed too high to put some distance between me and Mom and Dad, who were still coming to terms with their hasty decision to leave behind all they had formerly known and leap into a busy retirement here in the great sandbox at the end of the world. The house they lived in, larger than the cabins, was, I felt, still much too small for three people all freaking out in their new homeland.

So, in return for a summer's worth of painting shacks and

dealing with the plumber (who might just have to move in himself to get all these sinks and toilets fixed), I got my own private space with a bathroom I could turn into a darkroom. It was the one good thing about moving from Boston. Of course, once the season was over and we boarded up the unheated cabins, I'd have to move into the bigger place. I just hoped I'd have made a few friends by then so I wouldn't have to spend the long winter sitting around the hearth with two bored ex-teachers jockeying for the right to help me with my homework.

I'd finished putting up the safelights in the bathroom that morning, the red bulbs that let you see what you're doing in a darkroom without ruining the photographs. The windows had all been boarded over for the winter anyway, so I just left the bathroom boards up. I'd rigged a hose from the bathtub faucet to an old Formica table that was now wedged tightly inside the tub: this was where I'd do the chemical baths. I hadn't quite figured out a spot for the enlarger yet, though. The bathroom was small, and the only other place for something as big as an enlarger was on a board or something over the sink. (I'd have to take showers up at Mom and Dad's, but I didn't want to block up my toilet, even if it didn't always flush right.)

I made myself a tuna fish sandwich and washed it down with Gatorade and a Hershey Bar. It was funny—my mother let me eat all kinds of sugary junk she'd *never* have bought for my older sisters. Of course, I was just a little kid when they were teenagers—Carrie and Jane are twenty-seven and thirty now—but their scenes of struggle are embedded in my memory. A box of doughnuts appears in the bread drawer. Mom reacts as though she's discovered a cache of heroin.

"Doughnuts! There are doughnuts in here!"

The villainous sisters are sneaking out the back door. "Carrie! Jane! Did you buy these?"

"Carrie did," Jane offers, always helpful.

"No!" Carrie says, then decides offense is wiser than defense. "Jane bought eclairs! They're in her bedroom!"

Mom's eyes sweep sadly across their broad shoulders and down to their slightly rounded bellies. She sighs. "You're such pretty girls. I just want you . . ."

"To be perfect. Well, we aren't, so you better get used to it." That would be Jane, the smart-ass.

Mom ignores her. "We'll just give the sweets to Kenyon. He *needs* the extra pounds."

I guess it's no wonder they couldn't stand me. I'd sit there stuffing their cream-filled goodies into my mouth while they cried and whined about what belonged to them. Not much, apparently. And they belonged to Mom, at least for a few more years. Even though she's not as vigilant with me, she still pushes and pulls, trying to turn me into the more standard type of my species, one of those known as *normal*. But who decides what's normal and what's not? Sometimes it seems like the "normal" box is way too small for real people to fit into.

I was sitting out on my back step letting the sun and the glistening bay hypnotize me, appreciating having the whole beach to myself, when Dad came walking slowly down the path toward Mockingbird. It would have made a good photograph—his bent back, the curve of the bay, the winding path. But not a happy one. I looked away until he got closer.

"I've got good news and bad news. But the good news is for you, and the bad news is for me."

He looked tired, and I could tell his back was still hurting him. His original plan had been to paint all the cabins himself, but he'd hurt himself unloading the U-Haul the day we moved in, and he hadn't really been able to do too much since. (Hence, my handyman status, my garbage-hauling job, and my roommate-free housing.) Dad was not happy about the situation. He'd been planning on a working retirement for years. "To get outside and do something physical," he'd say, flexing his puny muscles. "That's what I need!" But after forty years of sitting around on your butt, I guess you don't turn into a manual laborer overnight.

"No plumber?" I guessed.

He pointed to me to show I had it right. "Every toilet on the Outer Cape seems to be having a bigger emergency than ours. I finally got a guy to promise me he'd show up on Monday, so be sure you're here to meet him. I want you to keep your eye on him. Make sure he isn't reading magazines or taking a nap and charging us for the time. Name is Frank Cordeiro. From Provincetown. That Pete guy down the road says he's reliable. We'll see."

"He's probably okay. You got a recommendation."

Dad shook his head. "You never know. We're outsiders here. It's something I hadn't thought about before we came. People who live in a place all their lives feel funny about newcomers sometimes. I can tell. They don't trust us."

"So we don't trust them either? Sounds like a plan."

Dad scratched the back of his head and then laughed at himself. "Maybe you're right. I'm just being paranoid. Maybe I'll feel better about the whole thing once I can bend over and tie my own shoes again."

"Are we going to pick up the paint this afternoon?"

He sighed. "No. I called the place in Orleans, and it hasn't arrived yet. Apparently the shade of blue I chose for the doors and window frames had to be specially ordered. Which he didn't tell me when I picked it out, or I would have chosen something else!"

"Things aren't exactly falling into place, are they?"

He didn't answer me right away. He was looking out over the water with that sad smile he gets way too often lately. I hate to see that smile; it seems like it's saying, *What the hell am I doing?* or even, *I give up.* It gives me the creeps. I feel like my real father is disappearing, and this hopeless old guy is trying to take his place.

Finally he shook his head and looked at me. "I guess you have to expect setbacks on a big project like this. Anyway, you've got today and tomorrow off—that's your good news. But Saturday our first customers show up, and I want you around in the afternoon in case I need you. We'll put them in Eagle, Hawk, and Shearwater. Most reliable plumbing, and your Mom's got 'em clean as a whistle."

"With my help, don't forget."

"No, I don't forget it," he said, and I immediately regretted reminding him he couldn't work the way he wanted to.

"Maybe you should go lie down on that special mat Mom bought you."

He straightened up a little bit. "That silly thing doesn't help. Anyway, I feel better today." But as he limped back up the path to the big house, he didn't look any better. Sometimes I felt like I'd gotten a little cheated not being born until my parents were old. I saw some pictures once of them riding bicycles with my sisters when Carrie and Jane were kids. They looked so *young;* my mother had bl flipped-up hair and tight pants, and Dad had a fuzzy, black mustache. The picture shocked me—I never knew those people.

So, two free days. Big whoop. I'd really be able to have a great time with no money, no driver's license, and no friends. About all I could do was ride my bike around. I'd had that bike since I was about ten, and my legs had gotten so long that I had to be careful now not to bang my knees into the handlebars when I pedaled. I had to sit as far back on the seat as possible and stick my knees out to the side, which always made me feel like nothing else fit me right either. Like my pants were too short, and my shoes were too small. Which was usually true, too.

I hadn't actually done much exploring since we'd been here. We'd driven into Provincetown for dinner one night, but it was hard not to feel like just another tourist when the place was so packed with them. It was less crowded in Truro, but I didn't know where anything was. So I pretended I was just going to get on my bike and ride around, see where I ended up. I guess I knew all along I was headed for the dump.

If Razzle Penney hadn't been the only teenager I'd laid eyes on since my arrival, I don't think I would have gone back to see her. Like Mom said, she was weird. It was hard enough for me to talk to a more-or-less regular girl; I couldn't imagine having much to say to a shaved-headed dump-lover. In her favor, however, was the fact she'd actually *asked* me to come back and see her, so I knew she wouldn't groan in disgust when I showed up. "Oh, no, that *Kenyon's* here."

I think it would be easier to talk to girls if I knew what I looked like. I look in the mirror, of course, but I can't seem to see a whole person in it. I see my long neck with that big Adam's apple, or my dark hair curling around my ears again because I've put off going to the barber, or my sharp nose with a zit hiding in its shadow, or my bushy eyebrows hanging like awnings over my brown eyes. But I can't get the whole face to hang together long enough to decide if I look okay or not.

Of course I never see myself smile because it feels too stupid to smile at yourself in the mirror, like you're flirting with your twin. But Bethany, who's the girlfriend of my friend Alex in Boston, once told me I had a nice smile, so maybe I do.

I had a few crushes on girls back at the Hancock School— the private school I attended tuition free for my entire life because my parents were on the faculty—but I was never able to cough up more than the occasional "Hi," usually delivered in a voice quiet enough to be lost beneath the banging of locker doors. About the only girl I ever talked to much was Bethany. It was no problem to talk to her because I never had to come up with any conversation ideas; all she ever wanted to talk about was Alex. Which was easy, but not all that great for my ego.

Some guys seem to know naturally how to talk to girls, but for me it's like learning a foreign language. Sometimes I'll think up something very clever to say to a girl, but then, when she's actually there in front of me, the words disappear. I feel like I'm in a game, only I don't know the rules, or I'm in a play and I haven't learned the lines. We used to get a course catalog from a college night school in Boston, and I'd read over the list of classes. They had all kinds of dumb stuff like "How to Make Dried Apple Dolls" and "Learn to

Unclutter Your Closet and Your Life," but they never had the course I was looking for: "How to Speak to a Girl Without Turning Infrared, Saying Something Dopey, or Spitting Your Gum into Her Hair." That last thing never happened to me—it happened to some guy in a book I read, but I always think about it when I chew gum.

It wasn't that I was unpopular at Hancock—it was more like I was invisible. The only club I joined was the photography club, which had only three other members. We held one meeting a year to choose a president and a vice president (so we could have something to put on our transcripts), but other than that we were a bunch of solitary guys who preferred to use the darkroom when we could have it to ourselves.

By the end of last year I was starting to get sick of being such a nobody. Alex, who I'd known since preschool, suddenly had a life, and it didn't look so bad. It also didn't include me. Not that Alex would dump a friend, but when you've suddenly got Bethany hanging around your waist and planning every spare moment for you, there just isn't time to hang with your old friends.

Bethany sings and plays the guitar; she hangs out with the artsy, *I-am-so-weird* kids. Alex draws cartoons, so he fit in there pretty well too, especially after he bleached his hair and put a blue streak down the middle. They invited me to a couple of the parties and I tried to convince myself I could fit in too, but, honestly, they were just too over-dramatic for me. The last party I went to, the bathroom was tied up all night by a potential suicide (or maybe she'd just broken up with her boyfriend, but everybody was making a *huge deal* out of it). And then, as if that wasn't annoying enough, this girl comes up and stares into my eyes and tells me my ears are lopsided.

Which they aren't—that's just the kind of bizarre thing those kids like to say. To confuse you.

Consider me confused. Aren't there any other people on this planet like me? There never seems to be a place I fit in. Unless I'm alone in my darkroom, of course. But I don't think you can count it as fitting in if you're alone.

Maybe if we hadn't moved out of Boston, I would have felt more comfortable this year. Maybe it would have been my breakthrough year. Maybe I'd even have gotten a girlfriend. Well, forget that. Now I'll have to start all over from scratch without even Alex to help me.

Obviously, I was desperate enough to go searching for friends at the town dump. Not that I imagined Razzle was on the cutting edge of the local high school social scene, but that was okay. Since she'd asked me to come to the dump today, at least the heavy conversational work was on her shoulders. And since I certainly wasn't going to fall for such a strange girl, it should be relatively easy to practice talking to her so I'd be less of an amateur when I finally *did* meet somebody else.

She must have seen me cruise into the sandy lot—by the time I jumped off my bike in front of the Swap Shop, she was standing out front, hands on her hips again, waiting. Today the short shorts were red and the tank top was blue; the whole outfit looked worn out, like it had come from one of the bins inside. Her reddish-gold brush of hair looked like mowed autumn grass. All in all, somebody I'd rather photograph than talk to.

"I figured you weren't coming," she said. "It's two o'clock already."

"I'm here," I said, always quick with the obvious. "Got any

new junk?" I started up the ramp, but Razzle blocked my way.

"Don't leave your bike there," she directed. "Somebody'll think it's free and ride off with it."

"No they won't. I'll be . . ."

She stamped her foot impatiently. "I'm telling you, that bike is *gone* unless you bring it inside my office! Hurry up. I want to show you something."

Fine. I wheeled the bike up the ramp and through the entryway, back into the storage closet Razzle called her office. There was already an old table full of papers in there and a bunch of busted-up chairs, which left very little room for a bicycle. No matter how I turned it, the back end stuck out through the open door. Razzle shook her finger at the problem, turned around in a circle a few times, and then took a notice off the bulletin board—one about tai chi classes—and wrote on the back with a marker DON'T TAKE THIS BIKE!—RAZZLE. She taped the sign to the bicycle seat, looking pleased with herself.

"Okay, now come and see what I got today—it's a real *find*." I followed her flapping shoes back outside and around the corner of the Swap Shop. There, leaning at a 45-degree angle, was a large, wooden playhouse, or most of one anyway, the kind some rich kid might have, with a painted door and flowerboxes underneath real glass windows. There was a sign taped to the door: THIS IS MINE!—RAZZLE. Her name obviously carried quite a bit of weight out here in Dumpland.

She drummed on the tipsy roof and clapped her hands. "Isn't it great? Didn't I tell you Thursdays were always good? You never know *what's* gonna come in." She was beaming at the thing.

"Yeah, I guess. How come you want this, though? I mean, you'd have to bend over to get into it, and . . . there's no back on it." I was half afraid she hadn't noticed this slight imperfection, but, of course, she had.

"So? I can rig up something to close it off. It's got a *floor* in it. I can *sleep* in it if I want to."

I shrugged. "I guess so."

She picked up my tone. "Oh, no, you're one of *those*."

"One of what?"

She shook her head sadly. "A Perwim. I should have known."

"A Per . . . what? What are you talking about?"

"Perwim. A person without imagination. That's why I'll never be able to live anywhere but here. The rest of the world is full of Perwims." She sighed at my misfortune and drummed on the door of her new real estate.

"Just because I don't see what's so great about an old wrecked playhouse I have no imagination?"

"You said it." She was dancing around now, but not in any of the usual styles.

Not just a nut, but an annoying nut. "Well, you're wrong. It just so happens that I'm a photographer, a *good* photographer."

"Big deal. So, you have a good eye, or you know how to do some darkroom tricks; that doesn't mean you have an imagination."

"Darkroom tricks! You don't know what you're talking about. Have you ever even been *in* a darkroom?"

She was standing with the heel half of her flip-flops turned underneath the front of the shoes now, bouncing up and down on her toes. The way she never stopped moving some part of her body made me wish I'd taken Dramamine before coming over. "What difference does that make?" she said. "Anybody who can't see what's so good about having your own house, your own little place to sit and read and think, and fix up, and put your own stuff in, and be yourself, has *no* imagination."

Immediately I thought of Mockingbird. My own leaky little cabin. Well, sure, having your own space was important, but surely she could come up with something better than a three-sided, falling-apart playhouse. Any old bedroom was better than some broken toy, wasn't it?

I tried to divert the argument. "Look, I didn't say it didn't have *potential*. I just meant it's kind of a mess right *now*."

Razzle seemed to cheer up as quickly as she got angry. She grinned at her little house. "*Potential!* That's the word for it. Wait 'til you see what I can do with it—there'll be no place like it anywhere." She put her long arms around a corner and gave the place a quick hug.

A horn began honking, loud and long, and then a shout went up. "Razzle! Where the hell are you? I don't have all day!"

Razzle stormed around the corner of the shop; I followed more slowly. There was a filthy wreck of a pickup truck parked in front of the building, and the Unabomber was sitting in the driver's seat.

"I'm here! Jesus, you could get out and look for me like a normal person. You make enough noise to wake the dead." She turned to me. "This is my brother Ezra. He's gonna take the playhouse back to Billie's for me."

Ezra opened the creaky door and stepped out of the cab. "Who're you?" he asked me. Now that he was standing up I could see he was taller than the Unabomber, probably taller than a number of professional basketball players for that matter. It was the fuzzy beard and deep-set eyes that made him look like he'd just emerged from his one-room cabin in the woods, bent on mayhem.

"Ken. Ken Baker," I said.

"Kenyon!" Razzle shouted. "You told me Kenyon!"

"Well, yeah. But people call me Ken."

"Why? Kenyon's a better name than Ken. It stands out!"

Ezra shook his head. "God, Razzle, you got an opinion on everything. Even somebody's *name*."

"I always thought Kenyon was sort of a weird name," I said, more to Ezra than Razzle. He wasn't too interested, though. He went around to open up the back gate of the pickup.

"Weird is good," Razzle said. "People remember a name like Kenyon."

"Or Razzle," I said.

"Yeah! Don't you want people to remember you?"

I didn't have to answer that because Ezra started yelling again. "Can we cut the deep thoughts? Where is this stupid thing you want me to take home? If I'm late for work on account of you, Razzle, you're gonna pay me what I lose in tips."

"Oh, Ezra, stop being such a crabass." She grabbed his arm and pulled him around the corner to where the playhouse stood. His reaction was somewhat worse than mine.

"This piece of crap? It's all broken! You think Billie is gonna let you have this in her yard? You're outa your mind, girl."

"I'll deal with Billie. You just help me get it on the truck."

"She's gonna toast your ass this time," Ezra said, as he bent down to lift one end of the little house.

I pitched in too, since I was standing there. "Is Billie somebody you live with?"

I was beginning to think that Razzle's family might not be the usual sort.

"Billie's our gramma," Razzle grunted. "Everybody calls her Billie."

That damn house was heavy; the three of us working together could barely budge it. "Back the truck over here, Ez," Razzle ordered. "We can't carry it that far."

"Yes, Your Highness. Jesus, what I do for you."

"Oh, yeah, you're practically my slave."

I don't know how we got the thing into the truck. All I can say is, Razzle is stronger than her bony body makes her look. The house ended up lying on its face in the truck bed like an enormous wounded grasshopper, its broken sides sticking up in the air like bent legs.

Razzle wiped her hands on her shirt. "I'm gonna close up the Swap Shop. It's almost three anyway. You want to come to Billie's with us? You could help us unload."

"I've got my bike," I said, not quite sure if I wanted to continue this adventure. I had an image of Gramma Billie smoking a big cigar and twirling a six-shooter around her finger.

"We can throw the bike in the back," Ezra said. He hadn't been too interested in me up to now, so I guess he was worried about getting the playhouse out of the truck without a third person.

"Where is this place?"

"Just up over those dunes," Razzle said, pointing north.

"Really? On the ocean side? I didn't think there were any houses over there."

"There aren't many. From Billie's place all you can see are a few of the old dune shacks down the beach. She says we've got a million-dollar view," Razzle bragged.

"From a hundred-dollar house," Ezra added.

They climbed into the front of the truck. "Come on, Kenyon," Razzle said. "If you live in Truro and you haven't met Billie, you're still a tourist. You don't want to be a *tourist* all your life, do you?" She made it sound like a cross between grave-robber and public nose-picker.

Obviously nobody wanted to be a tourist. I got in the truck.

three

Ezra's truck lurched out of the dump parking lot onto Route 6, the main Cape highway, but we didn't go far before turning off again onto a sandy dirt road I'd never noticed before. Actually, it was more like an alley than a road, but that didn't stop Ezra from gunning the pickup like he was on a racetrack. I could hear the playhouse banging around in the back and imagined it smashing my elderly bicycle into one of Eddie's sculptures.

"Slow down, Ezra. You're ripping up the road," Razzle said. "Billie'll kill you."

"I told you, I'm late for work."

"What? You think PeeWee's gonna fire you? The restaurants are all begging for waiters—you could get another job in five minutes."

"I don't want to get another job, Raz. I like it at PeeWee's."

"Yeah, I know. You like rubbing butts with Mimi every time you pass her in the kitchen."

Ezra gave her a sideways grin and shoved his shoulder into hers. "You're just jealous *you* don't have anybody to rub butts with," he said.

Razzle's face heated up and she shoved him back. "You're full of shit, Ezra!"

You could tell by how fast she flared up, he'd hit the nail on the head. Ezra knew it too; his eyebrows arched, but he didn't push her any farther.

Their relationship was obviously in a different league from mine with my sisters. Carrie and Jane were so much older than me they primarily ignored me, or, at best, bossed me around. These two battled like siblings, but you could tell they were pretty close. I'd never have dared tell either of my sisters they were full of shit, and they would never have known to stop teasing me when I'd had enough. It took parental intervention to end their terrorism.

Around our house the battles usually began with Carrie whining that Jane had stolen something from her: a book, a blouse, a boyfriend.

"If you don't appreciate him," Jane would say, "you don't deserve him." Jane always had a good reason for her crummy behavior.

"Does Jim like you better than Carrie now?" I'd ask Jane, all innocence, trying to understand how this *going steady* business worked.

"No, he does *not*," Carrie would answer.

Jane's response to me was usually even less revealing. "Go away, Kenyon! You're a baby. You don't even know what we're talking about!"

Any five-year-old knows what you say to that. "You're not the boss of me!" And then you run like hell since, as everyone knows, the biggest one is *always* the boss.

But usually I let them flail away at each other undisturbed. It drove my mother wild. Sometimes she'd spend half an evening helping them sort through a crisis, and by the time she stopped by my bed for the ritual tucking in, all she could do was whimper. "Thank you, Kenyon, for being such an easy child. If I'd had another one like those two . . ." She'd shake her head and let me imagine what horrors would have befallen her then.

What choice did I have? I was good at being good. Quiet. Invisible. Now that I think of it, Dad was pretty good at invisibility too. It guess it was the talent my mother appreciated most.

Ezra's truck groaned up a short hill, and suddenly the scrubby pine trees gave way to beach grass and sand dunes, and beyond them the most amazing view of sky and ocean, both going on forever in incredible shades of blue.

"Wow, this beats our view," I said.

"There's our house." Razzle pointed to the left just as Ezra turned in that direction, off the so-called road and onto a rickety wooden path built above the sand. An old house with weathered gray shingles leaned toward the water like it was getting ready to catch a wave. The roof came to a point in the middle, with a chimney right on top, and there was a porch wrapped around the first floor with posts holding it up. The house looked like a merry-go-round on top of a sand dune, and, as we got closer, I was almost disappointed not to see ponies going up and down inside the pillars.

The wooden path came to an abrupt end about half a city block from the house.

"I guess we can unload the playhouse here," Razzle said. "It's not that close to Billie's house."

Ezra shook his head. "Way too close. Besides, everybody drives up here—she'll have a fit. I'm gonna back up. Put it near the rugosa roses—that's not too far to carry it, and it's at least partly hidden from the road."

Razzle thought it over. "Good idea, Ez. Sometimes you're not as stupid as you look."

He grunted and backed down the path until I saw the spot he meant. It would take some muscle to lug the broken-down hutch that far, but there was no getting out of it now. As soon as I jumped out of the truck I realized there was another obstacle this time too: sand.

"Jeez, how are we supposed to carry it through the sand?" I said. "It's hard enough just to walk!" The sand swallowed up my shoes with every step I took.

Ezra and Razzle both looked at me like I was speaking Finnish or Swahili. "Take your shoes off," Razzle said, obviously amazed I needed to be told. I noticed then that they'd both already kicked off their sandals and were sliding through the sand on tanned, leathery feet. I'd have to get new shoes for this new life I was now apparently living. I untied my sneakers and removed my sweaty socks, feeling ridiculously embarrassed until the sand coated my pale, smelly size twelves.

Ezra was up in the truck already, shoving the house from behind. I plodded up to help Razzle ease it down onto the path. I was beginning to wish I'd used the weight room at school last year so there might actually be a little strength in my stringy arm muscles. I could tell Razzle was handling more of the weight than I was, but I was doing my best. Which wasn't quite good enough: the playhouse fell the last ten or twelve inches and just missed amputating several of Razzle's toes.

"God! If I hadn't pulled my foot back at the last minute, I'd be minus one foot, Kenyon! Hold up your end, will ya?"

"I am!" I lied. Razzle rolled her eyes, but didn't argue.

Once the house was off the truck, our work went a little more smoothly, but it took the three of us ten minutes to wrestle the thing twenty yards off the path and into some scrubby bushes.

"Turn it so it backs up into the roses," Razzle ordered. "Then I won't even need a back wall."

Ezra grunted. "All this work for nothing. I'm not carting this out of here if Billie has a conniption fit."

"You worry too much, Ez."

"And you dream too much, Raz."

"Need a lift back to the highway?" Ezra asked me as he prepared to escape.

"No," Razzle answered for me. "He's gonna meet Billie, remember?"

He snickered. "Oh, yeah, *that'll* be a good time."

I shrugged. It's not like I had any other plan for the rest of the afternoon. I grabbed my bike out of the truck and began to wheel it up to the house, but it was too hard to roll it in the sand.

"You can leave it here. Nobody comes up here but people we know," Razzle said.

Just then the sky-blue screen door flew open, and a herd of dogs came bounding out, barking and panting, heading straight for us. There must have been a dozen of them, all sizes, more dogs than I'd ever seen in one place in my life. And not one of them on a leash. I stood still and closed my eyes, waiting for the attack, hoping that if I didn't move maybe they'd think I was already dead.

"What are you doing?"

I peeked through eyes that were narrowed down to slits. There was a large black dog sniffing my crotch and a little white one running in circles around my legs. The others were more interested in Razzle.

"I'm not too crazy about dogs," I said.

"That's obvious. You better get used to 'em if you're gonna hang around with me," she said. As though that was already a given. "They won't hurt you. They're Billie's babies, sweet and spoiled rotten."

I opened my eyes all the way and watched Razzle drop to her knees to hug a big yellow slobbering creature. "This is Randolph. He's our oldest dog. Thirteen this year, aren't you boy? Ever since Everett left, Billie gets herself a new dog at the shelter every year on her birthday. Twelve so far, but she's thinking maybe thirteen would be an unlucky dog so she might skip this year. Twelve is her lucky number anyway."

"Who's Everett?"

"Billie's second husband. Not my grandpa—I never even met him. Grandpa Jacob was an artist—he just wandered off one day and never came back. Billie says we'd a' had to wait for hell to freeze over before Everett woulda wandered off— he hardly ever even got up off the couch—so one day she got tired a' waitin' and threw his sorry butt out. I don't remember much about Everett. Ezra says he watched TV a lot and didn't work much. After he was gone, Billie said she was through with men—dogs were more reliable. Everett hated dogs, so in honor of his leaving Billie got Randolph and fell in love. That was the beginning. Kneel down and get to know 'em, Kenyon. You don't want a bad reputation like Everett had."

I got slowly to my knees. The crotch sniffer had gotten his nostrils full, I guess, but the little squeaky dog was still hanging around me. I put out a hand to touch the raggedy thing, and it jumped right into my arms.

"That's Betsy-Wetsy. She likes you."

"Great. I hope she doesn't live up to her name." Betsy proceeded to clean my chin for me, squeaking happily.

"Not anymore. She's a lot calmer now than when we got her."

"Hard to imagine." Now that the dogs were used to us being there, they'd mostly wandered off, drinking from a big pail by the door or flopping down on the shady porch to rest. It felt sort of like standing in the jungle with Jane Goodall, holding the baby ape while the rest of the gorilla family goes about its business. They seemed calm, but how could you tell for sure? Meanwhile Ms. Goodall and Randolph were busy grooming each other.

"Do you know all their names?" I asked my fearless leader.

"Of course I do. How else can you talk to them? Ruby is over there by the chair—asleep as usual—and the little orangey one next to her is the baby, Peaches. Clementine is the black lab, and the greyhound that went back inside is Shimmy—he's very shy." She went on to give names and characteristics for all twelve as though they were her dearest friends.

I could hear my mother's reaction to twelve dogs in one house. "That's a public menace! It's unsanitary! Dogs running in packs become wild!" But these guys weren't running anywhere. Especially Betsy-Wetsy, who resisted my attempt to put her down by burying her snout in my armpit and whining.

"Either you smell like bacon or she's in love," Razzle said. "Bring her in the house with you."

We were almost to the door when Ezra came running up behind us. "I gotta call PeeWee and tell him I'm still coming.

It's so damn late he's likely to get Mike in to replace me tonight."

But when we walked in the door, the phone was already in use. A tall, stout woman in jeans and a lavender T-shirt that said I THINK I PUT MY SHIRT ON BACKWARD stood yelling into the receiver. A thick gray braid reached to the middle of her back, as much hair loose around its edges as captured in the weave, and a pair of red-framed glasses perched on top of her head. She didn't look like any grandmother I'd ever seen. She didn't sound like one either.

"I don't want her here and she knows it. Every time she shows up all hell breaks loose. Goddammit, I've already raised her, two husbands, two grandchildren, and a dozen dogs. I'd like a little peace!" The screen door slammed behind us, and she turned around, startled.

"Who?" Razzle asked. "Is Rusty coming?"

"God, I hope not," Ezra said. "I gotta use the phone, Billie. Right now!"

Billie waved at both of them to be quiet and turned away. "I can't talk now, Dell. The kids are here. Yeah, I'll let you know. Okay Bye."

"Is it? Is it Rusty?" Razzle asked again. Ezra grabbed the phone to call his boss.

"Hello to you, too," Billie said. "Could we act like we're halfway civilized and not yell questions at each other the minute you walk in? Who's your friend here?" She looked at me sideways as if she wasn't all that thrilled to see a skinny kid with big white feet standing in her house.

Razzle was pouting and seemed to have forgotten about me. "I'm Kenyon Baker," I said. "I was at the dump and . . ." Fortunately I remembered *not* to mention the playhouse.

". . . and Razzle wanted me to come here and meet you. I just moved to Truro."

She nodded. "You like dogs, I see."

Betsy had turned herself over on her back in my arms so I could scratch her stomach. I had to admit this one was growing on me. "Yeah, I do," I said, exaggerating just a bit.

She nodded again. "One point for you." For some reason I didn't think I'd be awarded many more.

"Kenyon's parents bought the Landmark Cottages," Razzle said, bouncing on the seat of a threadbare wing chair. "They're fixing 'em up. Moved here from Boston." She was anxious to get done with my introduction so she could get back to her immediate concern.

Billie stuck her hands deep into her jeans pockets and looked at me straight this time. "Good investment if they know what they're doin'. People come from the city, they don't always understand how to do things here. It's different."

I nodded. *She* certainly was different. Not only did she seem too young and energetic to be a grandmother, but there wasn't a trace of that aren't-we-all-nice voice that older people resort to when they don't know what to say to teenagers. I had a feeling Billie talked to everybody the same way.

"Some folks think if they buy a little sand and water they'll make a killing," she continued. "But if you don't know what you're doin', sand and water'll kill you first. If your folks came because they can't get the Cape Cod sand out of their shoes, they'll do okay."

"Billie, don't lecture him. God, they just moved here." Razzle was restless. She got up and went to the refrigerator, an old one that was barely as tall as she was. "What's there to drink?"

"Sun tea out on the front porch," Billie said.

"That'll be hot," she complained.

"Not if you put ice in it."

She slammed the fridge door. "Billie, just tell me—is Rusty coming?"

Billie sighed. "You gotta know everything, dontcha? I got a letter this morning. She wants to come next week."

"Tell her there's no room," Ezra said on his way out the door. "I'm sick of giving up my bedroom every time she feels like flopping here."

"I might just do that," Billie said.

"You can't!" Razzle said, hands flying to her nonexistent hips. "She's your daughter! She's our mother! And I like it when she comes. She's cool, and she's been all over, and . . ."

"And she fills your head fulla all kindsa crap and nonsense. She's a bad influence." Billie pulled a strand of loose hair into her mouth and chomped down on it.

"No, she isn't! Anyway, she doesn't *influence* me; she just tells me stories."

"Call it what you want."

"Please, Billie, say she can come!"

Billie stared out the door, like there was something fascinating going on out there on the dune. "I'm not making any decisions this minute. I'm going out to feed my dogs." Betsy's ears perked up when she heard that, and she struggled in my arms until I put her on the floor. Billie headed out the door with Betsy right under her feet, then remembered me and turned back briefly. "Nice to meet you, Kenyon. Now that you've seen our nuthouse, come back any time."

"Thanks," I said to the back of her backward shirt. I wasn't sure I wanted to take her up on her offer, though. I mean, she was sort of cool, but how were you supposed to act around adults who didn't follow the usual rules? Being a Good Boy seemed particularly dorky under the circumstances.

Razzle was distracted, thinking about her mother coming, I guess, so I took the opportunity to look around the room. It was quite something—one big kitchen and living room space all sort of mixed together. Loads of furniture that looked like it was either original to the house or had come from a flea market. Or maybe, now that I thought of it, the dump. It reminded me of the old stuff my grandmother had in her attic that had belonged to *her* mother: fancy, hard-backed couches with springs poking up from under the seats and stuffing breaking out around the edges, mushy chairs covered in fabric so old it had hardly any color left anymore, lots of hassocks and scuffed up old tables overflowing with magazines and knickknacks, and pictures everywhere, crumbly, old photos of people who must have died ages ago.

But in Billie's house there was another layer over the top of that one. Sort of as if the Woodstock Nation had taken over Grandma's attic. One wall had a huge American flag hung across it with a poster of a mostly naked Jim Morrison tacked in the middle of it. Multicolored Christmas tree lights were strung from the back door across the top of the kitchen windows and then disappeared into a room curtained off with Indian bedspreads. Bookshelves buckled under the weight of tons of ancient books, and more were piled in tall stacks next to chairs. There were pillows all over the floor and candles all over the tables, and incense burning away on a fireplace mantel lined with birds' nests. As a matter of fact, the house was so overcrowded with *stuff*—dog toys, soda cans, dead flowers in vases, dirty dishes, dropped shoes, guitar cases, driftwood, unidentified standing objects—you couldn't see the surface of most tabletops, and you could barely even find a path to walk through the place.

"Whataya think?" Razzle was watching me look around.

"Wow."

"Yeah, it's a disaster, but we like it. Billie was a hippie."

"Your grandmother was a hippie? How old is she?"

She shrugged. "Not that old. Fifty-four or five. I forget."

Younger than my dad. Not only were my parents older than my friends' *parents*—now they were older than my friends' *grandparents.*

"Come see my room," Razzle said. I followed her into the room that was hidden behind the bedspreads, a long, narrow space lined with windows, more like a porch than a bedroom.

"It *is* a porch," she said. "There's not even any heat in here."

"No heat?"

"It's not a problem. I've got a space heater for the coldest days. In the summer I have to keep the curtains pulled or it gets too hot."

And then I noticed all the containers—bags, baskets, packages—lining the floor of the room, piled neatly one on top of another. All of them full of . . . things. Sort of a miniature version of the rest of the house, except more neatly organized. Shells and rocks and sea glass and feathers, the kinds of things you might expect to find at a beach house, but other stuff too: beer bottle caps in one bowl and plastic milk caps in another, rubber bands and pieces of ribbon, stamps and buttons, postcards and photographs. There were buckeye buckets and jewelry jars, cups full of broken crayons and boxes full of broken dishes. Fabric, thread, plastic flowers, key chains, small toys, nails, pins, paper clips—everything sorted and easily available. But for what?

"You're staring again," Razzle said.

"Sorry. What's all this stuff *for?*"

"For when I need it. When I want to make something."

"Like what? What do you make?"

"Stuff. I don't know. Don't you ever *make* stuff?"

"Just photographs."

"Oh, yeah, I forgot. You're a photographer, which you think means you have an imagination." She grinned.

"And you don't."

She shrugged. "We'll see. Hey, how about taking pictures of me? I'm a good model. I posed for this photographer up on Peekshill Road one time. He said I was photogenic." She struck a pose and stared out the window, demonstrating her style. I had to admit she'd make an interesting subject, the bony angles and weird hair and all.

"Sure, I guess. Sometime."

"When?"

"I don't know. I have to get my stuff set up first." I never liked being pushed into things; Razzle's enthusiasm made me want to back off a little. Besides, photography was kind of a secret thing for me. I loved doing it so much it was almost embarrassing. It was too important—sometimes I thought it was the only important thing about me.

"Well, let me know when you're ready."

"I will." I sifted my fingers through a box of smoothly worn beach glass, soft blues and greens and ambers. "So where does your mother live?" I asked, mostly to change the subject. "Doesn't she get along with your grandmother?"

Razzle didn't answer right away. She picked up the cord

that opened the dusty green drapes and rolled it between the palms of her hands. "Rusty likes to travel. She only comes here when she's in trouble or broke or something. She's fun sometimes, but I don't really think of her as my mother—she doesn't act like a mother. She and Billie—I don't know—something happened. They don't talk about it in front of me and Ezra, but they just don't get along."

"Yeah, I got that."

She held her right hand up, palm toward me, as if she were taking an oath. "Here's the only thing Rusty ever gave me."

I stared at her hand. "What?"

She pointed to a small brown spot on the pad of skin beneath her thumb. "This mole. It was *hers.*"

I laughed, not certain what the joke was. "It was *hers?*"

She nodded. "Billie says it's true, too. Rusty had a mole right here on her hand, in the same place—then, after I was born she noticed one day it was gone. It wasn't on her hand anymore—it was on mine. Weird, huh?"

"That could really happen?" I said.

"Could? It did! Don't you believe me?"

"I've never heard of such a thing."

She snorted. "Perwim."

"Come on. A mole can't jump from one person's hand to another's."

"I didn't say it jumped. It *passed* to me."

Stupid as it sounds, I got a little chill when she said that. The whole place was so strange—what did I know about what could or couldn't happen to people like this?

I tried to get a more normal conversation going. "When did your mother move away? Does your father live around here?"

"Jesus, you're nosy!"

"I just wondered. Don't tell me if you don't want to."

She sighed. "My father left around the time Rusty did. I don't know much about it. I never met him. I don't even know . . . who he is."

I knew I should shut up, but it kind of shocked me. "You don't even know his *name?*"

Suddenly her eyes turned muddy and mean. "Whata you care?" She headed back through the curtains into the main room, and I figured she was mad, but then she turned back and flicked her tongue at me like one of those high school vampires on *Buffy.* "Did you know that the strongest muscle in the whole body is the tongue? You wouldn't guess that, would you?" She let the bedspread/curtain drop between us.

"What?" I followed her into the main room.

"I read it somewhere. I don't think it's true, though, for people who don't talk much, like you. If the tongue was your strongest muscle, you'd have to be carried around in a basket."

"Thanks a lot! I talk! You just told me I ask too many questions."

She picked up a box of matches from a table and lit half a dozen fat candles that were stuck to the wood with their own wax. "Yeah, you ask *questions,* but you don't say anything about yourself. You keep that stuff a big secret."

"I do *not!*"

She passed her index finger through the candle flames, closer and closer to the wicks. "Then tell me something. About you. Something secret."

I laughed uncomfortably. "I don't have any secrets." At least not any I was planning to impart to this kook.

"Oh, come on. Something you don't tell many people

then. Something that will show me who the *real Kenyon* is." She licked her candle finger, backed up into an overstuffed chair, and slid down into it so she was sitting sideways, her knees over the arm, long legs crossed, bare feet kicking the air.

It had never occurred to me before to want a tan. Getting one is such sweaty work, it doesn't last very long anyway, and then you get skin cancer. Why bother? But seeing the smooth dark brown of Razzle's legs, her sandy, summer feet, I wanted one too. It made her seem strong and capable and sure of herself. It also occurred to me that she was trying to look sexy; but it wasn't really working.

"Okay here's my secret," I said. "I was an accident."

She looked puzzled. "You were in an accident?"

"No, I *was* an accident. You know, a *surprise,* as my mom puts it."

The light dawned. "Oh, you mean your parents didn't plan on having you?"

"Right." Why was I telling her this? I never told anybody this kind of stuff.

But Razzle just shook her head. "You'll have to do better than that. Half the people I know, their parents aren't even married. My parents never were, either."

"Really?"

"You're on the Cape now, buddy. That kind of thing is not big news." She sighed. "I can see you're not in my league when it comes to secrets, but I'll tell you one anyway. My mother's name is Rosalind Penney, but in high school they started calling her Rusty because she liked to do it in the shower or the bathtub, sometimes even the ocean. And you know what happens to a penny when it gets wet."

Her look was so innocent that it took me a minute to figure out what she meant, and then I'm pretty sure I blushed. I laughed too, though, so she knew I got it. "This is the mother who's coming here?"

"I've only got the one. The thing is, she liked being called Rusty. She enjoyed her reputation." Razzle shook her head. "That's not really a secret, though, just news to you. Most people know all about it. Billie pretends she doesn't know where the nickname came from, but she's not that dumb. She thinks she's keeping it a secret from us, me and Ezra, but some kid told me about it in the sixth grade. Not such a great year for me."

What was I supposed to say to that? "I guess not." I stuck my hands in my back pockets wishing I still had the little dog to play with, so I wouldn't feel so awkward just standing around.

She sighed again. "Am I freaking you out? Do you want to leave? You can. I have to make dinner for me and Billie, and you probably wouldn't like what we eat."

Now she was kicking me out! I guess I wasn't weird enough or funny enough or something.

"I told my parents I'd be back by dinnertime anyway." Not true. If I didn't show up at the big house for dinner they'd just assume I was eating a sandwich at Mockingbird. Since I never gave them anything to worry about, they directed their anxieties into other arenas.

"Billie doesn't like men, but she didn't mind you too much. So you can come back, if you want to. You don't have to, though."

Billie didn't mind me *too much*—another fine compliment. "Well, maybe I'll see you at the dump sometime."

"Okay. Whatever." She didn't get up or look at me as I went to the door; she was pretending to pick lint off her shorts.

"Well, good-bye, then," I said.

"Bye. Oh, hey, Kenyon?" She was looking at the ceiling, her bony chin pointing toward my face. "Did you know that humans and dolphins are the only species that have sex just for the fun of it?"

Probably this was not a question she expected me to answer. I backed out the door with a weak wave, curious if perhaps all the dust and dog hair in that place could be gumming up her brain. It seemed to me she might need a good vacuuming out.

four

On Saturday morning our first guests arrived. In Eagle and Hawk were two couples from Boston who knew each other; they both had little babies, and I guess they just wanted something different to look at while they stayed up all night listening to their kids cry.

An old woman came by herself to stay in Shearwater. I carried her stuff into the cottage for her and couldn't help noticing she'd brought a paint box and an easel. The whole peninsula seemed to be full of people who'd taken up painting landscapes after retirement, and it definitely blew the theory that we could all be creative if only we had the time for it. I figured she was one of those; she'd no doubt dribble out a few pastel canvases of sailboats at sunset before she left next week, and all her friends back home in Pennsylvania would admire them and think of her as an artist.

I guess the idea galled me because, more than anything, I wanted people to admire *me* and think of *me* as an artist. I never told anybody that, of course. But every time I look through the lens of my camera and see how different the world looks when I frame it, when I choose what to leave out and what to put in—every time I click the shutter on the small, perfect world I've just put in order, I think, *I'm a pho-tographer.* I know it's sort of egotistical to think you're a real artist when you're still a kid and nobody else thinks you are. But you can't help the way you feel.

For some reason I'd gotten it into my head that once I moved the guests in, I'd have the rest of the weekend to myself. By mid-afternoon the tide was way out, and the sun made the sand flats ripple like corduroy and gleam like silk. I couldn't wait to get my camera and start figuring out angles.

"Where do you think you're going?" Mom said as I headed for Mockingbird.

"I'm done," I said. "I lugged the suitcases, hung towels in the bathrooms, and gave everybody trash bags and a tide schedule."

She shook her head. "You and I have to scrub down the last three cottages today and tomorrow so you'll be free to stay with the plumber when he comes on Monday."

Free to stay with the plumber? An interesting way to put it. This was going too far. "Mom!" I complained, "I haven't even taken my camera out of its case since we've been here. It's not fair!"

She sighed. "Please don't turn into your sisters the minute you hit sixteen, Kenyon. *Please.* I thought you understood the deal we'd made here. You get a cabin of your own for the summer in return for which you help us get this place up and running."

"Yeah, but don't I get any time off? What good is having my own cabin if I have to work around the clock?"

"Things will settle down once the places are all open. Besides, what do you have to do today that's so important?"

"Take pictures!" I said. I pointed to the slippery sand flats where the sun was now making perfect shadows. "I want to take this. Look!"

She looked, but I think her mind was already gathering scrub brushes and water buckets. "Kenyon, these flats will be here every day for the rest of the summer. For the rest of our *lives!*" She sounded as though the idea didn't thrill her.

I learned the hard way that with photographs, you don't usually get a second chance. You need to be on the lookout for great pictures and take them before they get away. "But the way they look now . . ."

She shook her head in that way that means, *I'll never understand you.* "I hate arguing, Ken. You know that. Run in and get your camera if you must. Take a few shots, and meet me at Loon in fifteen minutes."

I watched her trudging down the beach as if her feet were sinking into mud instead of sliding through sand. Fifteen minutes? What good was fifteen minutes? I looked at the flats again, begging the sun and wind and tide to all perform the same magic for me on a day I could photograph them for as long as I pleased. As for today, I might as well start scraping mold off windowsills.

By Sunday afternoon we were scrubbing the salt spray off the windows in Plover. My fingers were as pruney as old hotdogs, and the heels of my hands were numb. Mom had finally gotten sick of listening to Gilbert and Sullivan operettas on her portable CD player, thank God, and I was letting the silence lead me into a pleasant daydream in which I had my darkroom completely set up and was actually printing pictures.

But not for long; Mom wanted to talk. "So what do you think, Ken? Did we make the right decision?"

For a minute I was lost. I stopped pushing my newspaper wad and looked at it. "What decision?"

"You know, moving here. Giving up our life in Boston. Taking such a leap."

I shrugged. "I don't know. I thought you guys were all excited about moving here."

She scrubbed hard at a big splatter of gull poop. "We were. I guess we still are. But now, with your dad's back acting up, I don't know when he'll be able to do the heavy work around here. If ever. If we have to pay carpenters and painters and plumbers for everything . . ."

"He'll get better—it's just a strain."

She squinted her eyes at the spot on the glass. "Maybe. We're not getting any younger, though. I think that's what we thought would happen—we'd move out here and suddenly we'd be thirty again. Instead we just replaced our old problems with a whole set of new ones." She sighed. "Ignore me. I'm tired."

I didn't really feel like having a conversation, but since she sounded a little down I decided to make an effort. "I met this woman the other day—her name's Billie—and I was telling her about how we bought this place, and she said that if you guys had Cape Cod sand in your shoes, it would all work out. Whatever that means."

"It's a saying they have out here. Once you get Cape Cod sand in your shoes, you'll always come back. Doesn't mean you have to stay, though." Suddenly she stopped scrubbing and gave me a funny look. "What woman? Where did you meet some woman you were telling our life story to?"

"She's not just some woman; she's Razzle Penney's grandmother. You know, the girl I met at the dump?"

She kept staring at me until her memory clicked in. "That *weird* girl? When did you see her again? And how did you meet her grandmother?"

"I went up to their house Thursday—it's not that far from the dump."

She grabbed a fresh piece of newspaper and crumpled it up. "Kenyon, I don't like you hanging around with that girl."

"Why? You don't even know her!"

"I know the type. She's got a chip on her shoulder. You'll make better friends when you've been here a while."

"She's okay when you get to know her."

Her nose twitched as she continued the inquisition. "And why are you calling the grandmother by her first name?"

"Everybody calls her Billie—Razzle said so."

"Well, I don't like that either. You don't call an elderly woman by her first name."

"She's not *elderly*. She's younger than Dad."

"She told you her *age?*"

I picked up my bucket, my sponge, and my newspapers and moved around the side of the cottage to do the little bathroom window. I couldn't even figure out what she was getting so steamed about. Ms. *Don't-Argue-With-Me*.

It's not like I was crazy about Razzle myself, but the idea that Mom wanted to ban me from seeing her just because Razzle didn't fawn over her like those phony girls at the Hancock School who called her the Spanish Flu behind her back . . . well, it stunk.

We washed windows in silence for about ten minutes, but I knew Mom was still thinking about it—I could feel her anger and anxiety blowing around the corner like the first winds of an approaching storm. And I could feel myself getting tense, waiting for the bolt of lightning and wondering where it would strike. Then, all of a sudden, she was standing there, just a small, gray cloud, looking worried.

"You're such an innocent kid, Kenny. That's what worries me. You lived in a protected world in Boston."

I threw the sponge into the bucket and soapy water splashed my jeans. Enough was enough. "What are you talking about? Our house was broken into last year! That nut job spit at me on the subway! Our neighbor's dog got shot in her front yard! That's why you wanted to leave, remember? To go someplace safe."

"I mean you've been emotionally protected. You haven't had a lot of friends . . . or relationships."

"You think I don't know that? That's why I'm trying to meet people here." Did parents really think it helped to continually point out your weaknesses?

"I'm just saying, people out here are different from the ones you're used to."

"I know they're different! I'm glad they're different!"

"Stop yelling, please."

Impossible, just now. "I don't need to be emotionally protected!"

"I saw that girl. She's not like the girls at the Hancock School. And now you're telling me that both her mother *and* her grandmother obviously had their children when they were about eighteen years old. That is who she *is!*"

"You mean, as opposed to the girls at the Hancock School who had abortions when they were eighteen years old?"

"Oh, Ken. I don't want to argue about this; I really don't."

"Then go back to your side of the building and wash the windows."

I never spoke to my mother like this. There was never any reason to. I didn't give her any trouble—she didn't give me any. But now, the first time I stepped a little bit outside her carefully drawn lines, she went ballistic on me. I didn't deserve it.

She pursed her lips and I knew she wanted to say more, but now she was angry, and she didn't like to be angry. "Just be careful, Ken. That's all I'm saying."

I grunted at her and moved down to soap up the bedroom window. I wasn't used to feeling angry with my parents. Amused, yes. Even disdainful. But not this thick, hot, mean feeling. I tried to push it aside and calm down, but it wasn't easy. Finally Mom stopped looking at my head, trying to read my mind, and went back to her own pane of glass.

I know the type. Her words repeated in my head. I didn't know she had prejudices like these. I'd never noticed it around Hancock. Of course, we weren't really very different there; even the scholarship kids were mostly white and middle class. But now, out here, she'd become this nervous person who was willing to stereotype Razzle based on some idea she had about girls who stand up to adults, or work at dumps, or call their grandmothers by their first names. She didn't know about Ezra, or Rusty, or the playhouse, or the bags of shells and buttons. There was a lot going on with Razzle, I thought, although I didn't really understand her myself.

I supposed she was a little nuts, but it was fun to be with somebody who was unpredictable. I'd never known anyone like her before. Besides which, she was the *only* person I knew around there. And as for being a hermit all summer—been there, done that. I wanted to meet kids and make a new start in Truro, where nobody knew I was Mr. and Mrs. Spanish Flu Baker's geeky son.

"Young man!" I turned around to see the old lady from Shearwater coming toward me. Mrs. Thackery. What did *she* want?

"I was just wondering if there might be another lamp available for me to use while I'm here?"

"Doesn't Shearwater have two lamps?" I didn't smile.

"Oh, yes, it does," she said, with a happy laugh. "One in the living room and one in the bedroom. But, you see, I really like to paint at night, in artificial light. I know it sounds silly—most artists come down here to use the marvelous seacoast light in the daytime, but I just need the smell of the ocean to inspire me. I paint the *aroma*. I like to stay up late at night working, then sleep most of the day. So a third lamp would be a big help, if that's possible."

Jeez, nobody down here was who you thought they were going to be. Or maybe they just turned weird when they hit Cape Cod. Maybe back at home Mrs. Thackery was as normal as fudge.

"Sure. I can take a lamp out of Egret, next door to you. There's nobody in there right now."

"Oh, that would be so wonderful! Thank you. And once I'm all set up you can come and watch me if you want. I *love* an audience!"

Razzle, I thought, would probably like Mrs. Thackery.

five

It was before eight in the morning when Dad started hammering on the door of Mockingbird. I was in the middle of a weird dream where Mrs. Thackery was painting a portrait of Chelsea Clinton and I was cleaning out her brushes for her. We had to keep telling Chelsea not to get up and walk around—she was having a hard time sitting still.

The reason I was too tired to get up had to do with Mrs. Thackery too. I'd been sitting out on the sand counting stars the night before around midnight and noticed the light on in her window. She'd said I could come by and watch her paint, so I thought I'd just go over and see what kind of funny stuff she painted in the middle of the night with only the smell of the ocean for inspiration.

I ended up staying until about three o'clock in the morning. Mrs. Thackery wasn't painting Chelsea Clinton; she was painting herself. At least, that's what she said—the faces didn't really look like her, or even like faces. She worked quickly, big strokes on large canvases with lots of dark purple tornado shapes surrounded by wispy white feathers that could have been her hair. She started three paintings in three hours. That's how she works, she said—she starts with quick bursts of energy and then slows down as she goes along, making changes until she's happy with the picture.

It was kind of exciting. I've never heard anybody talk about painting before. Not that Mrs. Thackery is a blabbermouth or anything. Mostly she worked silently, but every now and then she'd remember I was there and tell me stuff like why she'd just added a new color or painted over something. I liked hearing somebody talk about making that kind of decision. It's the same in photography. You make choices based on what you're feeling. It's not like math or even English, where you have to go by all these rules. You can make your own rules.

Anyway, it didn't occur to me that Dad and the plumber would really show up on time. I dragged myself out of bed and staggered to the door in my boxers.

"You're not up yet?" Dad said. "Didn't I tell you eight o'clock?"

I yawned. "Guess my alarm didn't go off."

The young guy with the show-off biceps standing behind Dad smirked. This was the plumber? For some reason I'd expected an old, stooped-over guy with a grizzly beard and skanky pants, not this raring-to-go jock in a tank top.

"Go get dressed. We'll wait." Dad ushered the plumber into my tiny kitchen area while I threw on a pair of jeans and a T-shirt and brushed my teeth. My eyes felt swollen, unwilling to take in the generous amount of sunlight pouring in all the windows.

By the time I came out, squinting, Dad had made a pot of coffee in Mockingbird's crusty old coffeemaker, one of my two appliances, the other being an equally ancient toaster. Mr. Plumber was drinking out of my favorite cup, the black one with the e.e. cummings poem on it in white print.

"Mind if I make a piece of toast?" I asked Dad.

"Go ahead. Just keep in mind we're paying Mr. Cordeiro

by the hour." He tried to make it sound like a joke, but he'd been so glum lately that it just sounded sour.

"Call me Frank," the guy said. "Mr. Cordeiro's my dad's name."

"Frank, then. I suppose you've gathered that this layabout is my son, Ken."

Layabout? Jeez, it's not even eight o'clock yet. And it's summer!

"Do you want to show me which cottage we're starting in," Frank asked Dad, "while Ken finishes his breakfast?"

Dad nodded. "Good idea. Ken, meet us down in Sandpiper as soon as you're finished."

Yeah, yeah. What was the big rush anyway? This guy was gonna be here for a while, wasn't he? Did I have to follow him around like a puppy every minute? He didn't look like the type to nod off after lunch, although I was hoping to try that myself.

By the time I got down to Sandpiper Frank had already brought in a bunch of tools, and Dad was telling him what was wrong in this particular cabin.

"I'll get the toilet working first," Frank said, "and then get the drains snaked out. Maybe it won't be as big a job as you think."

I knew exactly what Dad thought. He thought if this was the only plumber available on short notice there had to be something wrong with him.

"I guess I'll drive up-Cape this morning and pick up the paint," Dad told me. "Then you can get started on your job too." Terrific.

"I thought you wanted me to go with you. To carry it. Mom said I should."

He brushed my comments aside. "I'm okay. Your mother worries too much. Can't I carry a few cans of paint by myself?"

I wasn't going to be the one to tell him he couldn't. I hadn't been looking forward to the long, silent drive anyway. When Dad's upset, he gets quiet, but it's a mad quiet, and you start to feel like you've been sitting too close to a fire. Your skin gets hot, and your nerves feel downright scorched.

So what was I supposed to do now—just stand around and watch this guy work? Sandpiper had already been furiously bleached by my mother—no mere germ could have survived her attack. Still, I got out a sponge and pretended to clean the stove for about two minutes. Then I thought, what the hell am I doing this for? Old Frank's in the bathroom, and anyway, he doesn't care what I'm doing. So I just sat at the kitchen table and put my head down on my arms.

"Hey, Ken," Frank called from the bathroom. I lifted my head slightly.

"What?"

"You busy out there?"

I hesitated for a second. "Not really."

"Why don't you come in here and keep me company? I get sick of listening to the radio all day."

Great. Now my job was *entertaining* the plumber. I walked to the doorway. "I have to start painting when my dad gets back with the paint."

"He hasn't even left yet. I interrupted his breakfast. Sit down." He motioned to the lip of the tub. "Tell me about yourself. How'd your family end up out here?"

Just my luck to get stuck with a friendly plumber. He didn't seem like a bad guy, though, so I sat down. What else was there to do? "We moved here from Boston," I said.

"I know. Your dad told me the basics. Retired school-teachers. Vacationed here a few years ago. Still, buying a place like this, all the work involved, it's a lot to take on." As he talked he stuck a long tool of some kind down into the toilet and twisted it around.

"My mom says they bought it because they thought it would make them feel young again, but instead it just makes them feel older."

"That sucks. Maybe once your dad's back heals, they'll feel better."

"Maybe."

"What about you? You like it out here?"

I shrugged. "I guess so. I don't know many people yet."

"It's hard in Truro. There are the old-timers and the tourists and not much in between. You been to Provincetown yet?"

"Just one night for dinner."

He smiled. "That's the place, my friend. P-town. No place like it. I'll take you in with me after work some day, show you around."

"You always lived there?"

"I grew up there, but I left for a while when I was about twenty. Stayed away almost ten years. Some things were going on. . . . I had to get away." He pulled the tool out. "The clog's not in the bowl. I'm gonna have to dismount the toilet to get to the trap."

"But you came back," I said, to remind him what he was talking about.

"Hmmm?" He'd crawled down under the bowl to tighten or loosen some valve or bolt or something.

"You came back to Provincetown."

"Oh yeah. Cape Cod sand in my shoes." He grinned at me.

"Hey, is there a mop around here? This gets a little messy."

I went down to Plover, where Mom and I had left our cleaning supplies, and came back with a mop and a sponge, just in case. "How come you wanted to be a plumber?"

"Well, it wasn't so much I wanted to be a plumber as I didn't want to be a fisherman. That's what my family does. My dad, my uncles, my brother. I couldn't see myself sitting out on a boat soaking wet shucking scallops in lousy weather for the rest of my life. I had enough of that during my teens." He shook his head. "They still got their boat, the *Juliet,* named after my mother." He crossed himself almost absent-mindedly. "The fishing industry's ruined, though. I can make twice as much plumbing as my brother can fishing."

"Is your mother . . . ?" Maybe you shouldn't ask people stuff like that, but he seemed to like talking about himself.

"Yeah, she's dead. Cancer. About five years ago. That's why I came back, really. Dad used to call her 'Juliet my joy.' He loved her a lot." He laughed. "She called him Manny the Mouth 'cause he talked too much. I guess I inherited that, huh?"

I tried to imagine my parents calling each other names like that. Impossible. They stuck to the routine Ted and Mary Pat. *Periwims.* The word floated up like the right answer on a Magic Eight Ball. I shivered.

"Okay. Ready to move it. You gimme a hand?" Frank told me to hold the tank part, and he stooped low to pick up the bowl. God, he was strong, especially for a guy about thirty-five years old, which is what I figured he must be, what with the ten years away and the five years back. He looked a lot younger than that, but I guess that was because of the muscles and the tan and everything. He grunted and heaved while I pulled, and with a sort of pop the thing was up. We carefully moved it across the room, under the window.

Frank took a deep breath and kept on talking. "Manny, he remarried about two years ago. She's a nice woman, but she's no Juliet. I'm glad he didn't change the name of the boat, anyhow."

"Yeah, that's good," I agreed.

Frank looked out the window. "Hey, your Dad's just driving away now. It'll take him a good hour or more to get back with that paint. You wanna go take a nap in the bedroom? I'll wake you as soon as he comes back."

Okay, I did feel a little bit like a traitor. I mean, here I'm supposed to be watching this guy to make sure *he* doesn't go to sleep, and the first chance I get, *I'm* hitting the sack. I'd obviously already switched loyalties from Dad to some guy I met half an hour ago.

I don't know why, but I sort of trusted Frank Cordeiro. Maybe because he wasn't one of those hustler-type guys who's always trying to impress you. He was just who he was, a regular working guy who lived a regular life and was pretty happy about it. If Frank said I might as well take a nap, hey, who was I to argue?

Sprawled across the bare mattress, I was asleep before you could say *dismount the toilet*.

six

Frank woke me up the minute the station wagon came rumbling in the drive. By the time Dad started unloading the paint I was sprinting down the path toward him, his eager son, ready to help out. We stored most of the paint in the garage—it seemed to me it hurt Dad just to carry it that far—and I collected some brushes, rollers, and rags to take down to Sandpiper.

"Never got to finish my newspaper this morning. I thought when I retired I'd at least get to read the paper," Dad grumbled as he returned to the main house, but I knew it was actually his back that was annoying him.

I carried two gallons of white paint and one gallon of blue down to the cabin and set myself up in the kitchen. The insides of the cabins were to be repainted all white so they looked clean—at least for a little while. I didn't have to paint the outside shingles, thank God, since they were weathered clapboards, but I would have to do the trim. For some reason a lot of people on the Cape paint their window and door frames some shade of blue, so I guess Dad figured, when in Rome, buy blue paint.

It was an easy enough job. Newspapers on the floor, masking tape around the doors and windows, then slather on the paint. I figured it didn't need to be perfect—the tourists who stayed with us would be looking at the view, not the walls. By the time Mom brought down some sandwiches, I'd finished the little kitchen and started in on the bedroom.

"It's going pretty fast, huh?" She inspected the job. "Don't be in too big a hurry, Ken. These cabinets look awfully streaky."

"So, who'll notice?"

"*I'll* notice. Are you painting in one direction, like I told you?"

"Yes, Mrs. Baker," I said, hoping to remind her that I wasn't, in fact, one of her robot students. Mom had a reputation for being a strict teacher, but she'd always let things slide a little when she got home, especially for me, the one she raised on automatic pilot. I could see that having her around all day like this, as my *boss*, was obviously going to suck.

She set the sandwiches and a jug of lemonade out on the picnic table, then called into the bathroom. "I brought some for you too, Mr. Cordeiro, if you're hungry."

"Call him Frank," I said. Mom gave me a weird look as if I'd suggested she might want to go on a date with the guy.

Frank came out drying his hands on a rag. "Thanks, Mrs. Baker. I brought a lunch, but I might have some of that lemonade instead of more coffee."

"Help yourself. Ken, bring the leftovers back up to the house when you're done. And take your time with that painting. You're not in a race." She trudged away as Frank went to get his lunch box from the truck. I downed a whole sandwich before he reappeared.

"There's somebody out on the road looking for you," he said.

"For me? I don't *know* anybody."

"Guy in a black truck," he said.

Surely it was a mistake. But no, there sat Ezra banging the palms of his hands against the steering wheel, head bobbing to the music blaring from the radio. He was as incapable of being quiet as his sister.

"Razzle wanted me to check if you'd be around later, after the Swap Shop closes," he said.

"I'm pretty much always here."

He didn't take me up on that point. "Okay. I guess she might ride over or something. On her bike."

"Okay."

"She wanted to give you an advance warning, in case you want to escape or anything."

Escape from *here,* or escape from *her?* "I'm working. I'm painting the cabins."

He nodded. "I'll tell her."

"Thanks for letting me know," I said, backing away from the truck. Ezra just sat there, enjoying Led Zeppelin, obviously in no hurry to leave. They were more than strange, these two. Was he waiting for me to say something else? What?

"Yeah. You know. . . ." He stopped and looked out the other window, as if the motel across the road had suddenly captured all of his attention. Finally he continued, still not looking at me: "Razzle doesn't have a lot of friends."

"I didn't know that," I said. Although it wasn't a big shock.

He shrugged. "She's different."

I laughed. "Everybody around here's different."

He looked at me. "But Razzle's even different from *them.*"

What was I supposed to do with *that* information? "What do you mean?" I asked him.

He gave me a long look and then put the truck back in

gear. "Don't worry about it. See ya, Ken." And he spun off in a cloud of sand and pebbles.

Frank had finished his sandwich and was polishing off a yogurt when I got back. "Friend of yours?" he said.

"Sort of. Not exactly." I didn't feel like getting into it.

He finished his yogurt, lay back on the picnic bench, and closed his eyes. I hoped he wasn't going to fall asleep right out here where Dad could see me doing nothing about it.

"This is what I missed those years I was gone," he said.

I looked around. "The sun? You know, you can get that almost anyplace now. It's been imported."

He laughed. "Not just *any* sun, kiddo. *This* sun. Cape sun. Something about the way it slants in over the water. The smell of it. Not the same anyplace else."

"The lady in Shearwater says the ocean has an aroma. I don't think she means that dead fish stink, either."

"I know what she means. The sun, the ocean, the sand, the kelp, the scrubby pines, all of it together: the perfect smell."

I took a deep breath. "I don't think I smell it."

"You will. Sometimes it takes you washashores a little while to notice it. My guess is you're one of those people who'll get the scent caught in your nostrils and never be able to get it out."

"Sort of like the sand in my shoes?"

"Right. Now I'm just gonna take a ten-minute nap, and you're gonna let me know if you see your dad headed this way, Okay?" Almost immediately he started breathing in a deep, rhythmic way, fast asleep. Right out in the open. Terrific.

The bedroom took me longer. There must have been some kind of paneling underneath those thirty-eight coats of paint—something slick that made the paint bead up. I had to keep going over and over it. By the time Dad came down to check on my progress I'd only finished one wall.

"What's taking you so long? I thought you'd have this whole room done by now!" I sank down onto the mattress and explained the problem, how I'd gone over and over that wall to make it look as smooth as it did. "You're not painting the White House, you know. It doesn't have to be perfect!" he said, just to prove he hadn't spoken to my mother all day.

Frank came out of the bathroom. "The toilet's fixed, Mr. Baker, but you got a pipe rotted out under the sink. I'll have to go get another section to replace that."

Dad nodded. "Okay. It's after three already. You might as well wait and bring it tomorrow."

"Does that mean I'm off for the day too?" I said.

"You didn't get an early start like Frank did," Dad said.

At which point I looked out the window and saw her, Razzle, my skinny excuse, walking down the line of cottages toward Sandpiper, looking for me.

"Dad, see that girl? I sort of told her I'd be off at three. So we could . . . ride our bikes together." I stuck my head out the screen door and waved to her, and she slithered on toward us.

"I didn't know you'd made any friends yet," Dad said. But I figured he'd be glad I had one, even one as odd as Razzle. We stepped outside to meet her.

"Hey, Kenyon. You're here," she said, sounding surprised.

"I told Ezra I would be. This is my dad. Dad, Razzle."

"Razzle, did you say?"

"It means 'Angel of Mysteries,'" she told him, grabbing his hand firmly. "Nice to meet you." Frank joined us then, lugging his toolbox, and she gave him a big smile too. "Hi, I'm Razzle."

Frank stuck out his hand. "Frank," he said simply.

"So, am I off work?" I asked again.

Dad sighed, but there was a smile behind his eyes.

"We could go to Calderone's for ice cream," Razzle said. "It's just down the road. Ever been there?"

"No. Sounds good," I said, even though I'd passed the rickety shack more than once without the slightest desire to go inside. Still, any activity that didn't require a paint roller got my vote.

"You can cut out early today," Dad said. "But it won't be a regular thing. We've got an agreement." He kept sneaking glances at Razzle, trying to put it all together, I'm sure: the inch of hair, the gangly limbs, the tiny clothes, the enormous attitude.

"Help Frank put his things back in the truck, and then you're free," Dad said. "Have an ice cream for me." He seemed glad that at least somebody was going to have a little fun.

Razzle followed me into the bathroom and picked up a saw and a pair of safety goggles, leaving nothing for me to carry but a portable light Frank must have clamped onto the tub to see behind the sink. She strode out toward the truck.

"I never saw you before. I thought we'd had every plumber on the lower Cape up at our place. You live in Truro?"

Frank finished packing the truck. "Nope. P-town. Only been in business a few years."

"Oh, we'll get to you then."

Frank laughed. "So, you're going to Calderone's. I used to hang out there when I was a kid. With my Truro buddies. Great ice cream, but lousy . . ."

"French fries," Razzle said, finishing his sentence.

Frank nodded. "I guess some things never change. Which is nice to know, actually."

"You must work to get those muscles. And I don't mean plumbing. We never had a plumber who looked like you," Razzle said. I was just about to whisk her down to Mockingbird, embarrassed by her ogling of Frank's body, when she asked him a question that made me freeze in my tracks.

"So, are you gay?"

For just a moment, there wasn't a sound. At least not one I could hear, not a car on the road, not a gull in the sky, not a kid on the beach. Then Frank said simply, "Yeah, I am."

"I thought so," Razzle said. "I wasn't sure, but, you know, the muscles."

Then Frank really laughed. "Well, that's not always a guarantee, you know."

"In P-town it is. All the straight guys are pussies."

I could tell Frank was actually enjoying Razzle's outrageousness. But I was still reeling. How could she tell he was gay after only two minutes when I'd spent the whole day with the guy and didn't have a clue? I thought he was a tough-guy type. I went to *sleep,* for Christ's sake, in the next room. Not that I'd expect a gay guy to do anything to me, but I probably wouldn't have just crashed out right under his nose either, like an invitation or something.

I'd never known anybody very well who was gay. There was a lesbian teacher at the Hancock School, but I was never in her class. We'd had some gay neighbors in Boston, too, but I only saw them walking their dogs up and down the street. None of them looked like Frank. I knew Provincetown had a reputation for its large gay population, but I still didn't expect their *plumbers* to be gay.

I guess Frank could tell I was kind of stunned. "You okay, kiddo?" he asked.

"Sure. I'm fine."

"Maybe I should have mentioned it before, huh?"

"No big deal," I said, trying out a hoarse laugh.

He climbed into his truck. "See you tomorrow?"

"Yeah, see you then."

"Go eat an ice cream cone for me!" he yelled as he drove off.

I waved to him. Right. Now I was alone with the craziest girl on Cape Cod, and we'd promised to eat enough ice cream to satisfy everybody I knew. Fortunately that was a pretty small crowd.

seven

"I can't believe you just asked him right out like that. *Are you gay?* What if he hadn't been?" I said. We were pedaling the two crappiest bikes I'd ever seen down the road to Calderone's.

"Then he'd have said, 'No, I'm not.' Why are you so freaked out?"

"Because you don't just *ask* people stuff like that. It's rude."

"I don't think it's rude. Anyway, I was pretty sure he was."

"How could you be? I didn't know. How could you tell? And don't say *muscles*. Lots of people have muscles."

An oil truck rumbled past and I felt like I was being blown off the road, but Razzle didn't seem fazed by it.

"There's just something about him. He's very sexy in a way straight guys usually aren't. Unless they've got testosterone poisoning, and then they're annoying as hell."

For some reason I suddenly felt like a eunuch. Fortunately Razzle was already onto a new subject. "So when are you going to take photographs of me?"

"Did I say I would?"

"Remember, I told you, I was a model for a photographer once. I know how to hold still."

That could not possibly be true. Even while riding a

bicycle Razzle had to be constantly running her hand over her buzzed hair or rolling her head in a circle.

"You don't need to hold still. Unless the photographer is using a slow speed for some reason."

She wouldn't give up. "So, will you? I'm really photogenic. I have a good nose."

I rode up alongside her so I could get a look at the nose in question. It *was* a good nose, long and thin, like the rest of her. It seemed larger than it really was because the rest of her facial features were small. With the sun behind her, her nose threw angular shadows across her cheekbones. She was right—she'd be an interesting model.

"Okay. I don't have my developer set up yet, but I could still take some pictures."

"Really? How about tomorrow, after the Swap Shop closes?"

We pulled our bikes into the gravel drive that surrounds Calderone's and dropped them onto the sparse grass. "I don't know. My dad wants me to put in a full nine to five every day in return for having my own cabin for the summer."

"You're living alone in one of the cabins?"

I nodded. "Mockingbird. The bathroom is my darkroom, or soon will be."

"Wow. You can't give that up. How about if you start work earlier?" She did some quick calculations in her head. "If you started at seven o'clock and just took half an hour for lunch, you'd have eight hours in by three-thirty!"

"Seven o'clock? In the summertime?"

"It's cooler in the mornings anyway. I'm just trying to help you," she said as I followed her to the door of the shack. "You don't want to work all *day*."

I sighed. "True. I'll see what my dad says."

The inside of Calderone's was dark, especially after the glare of that special Cape sun. There was a counter on one side where two identical twin girls with backward baseball caps over ponytails scooped cones and took food orders. The place smelled like a hundred years of grease.

"Hey, Raz!" I turned around to see who'd called her, but my eyes were still adjusting to the darkness and all I could see was two dark shapes sitting at a back table.

"Hey, Primo," she said. Then, halfheartedly, "Harley." We ordered two large cones and were presented with monstrous towers of ice cream that began to run down our hands before we could gather enough napkins around the bottom to catch the overflow.

"Should we go sit with your friends?" I asked.

Under her breath, Razzle mumbled. "They aren't friends. At least, she's not." But then she reconsidered. "You don't know anybody—you should meet Primo. He's okay. Just watch out for *her*."

As soon as I saw who we were headed toward, I figured there was no way I would get along with Primo—he was a total punk. Of course, Alex looks punk now too, but when you've known somebody all your life you know what's under the costume. This kid had bleached blond hair with about half an inch of dark brown roots showing, and he'd gelled it up into a dozen peaks that stood straight out from his head. He was wearing the usual getup: big black pants, a heavy, choke-chain necklace with a padlock hanging from it, one dangly sperm earring, and a tight, black Operation Ivy T-shirt. While wolfing down a grilled cheese sandwich he scoped me out too, noticing, I imagine, that my shirt had no musical affiliation, my jeans fit, my hair was the plain old brown I was born with, and I was jewelry free.

It was hard to pay too much attention to Primo, however, when a girl like Harley was sitting across the table from him wearing a small, tight sweater stretched thin over the rolling hills. Harley reminded me of Natalie Wood in that old movie, *Rebel Without a Cause,* sort of bored and restless with good hair and a very pretty mouth. The kind of girl to whom I'm usually invisible.

Razzle made the introductions but didn't sit down, so I didn't either.

"So, Ken," Harley said, sipping a soda and leaning back in her chair as if she needed the distance to really look me over. Did this mean she could actually *see* me?

"Kenyon," Razzle repeated.

"*Kenyon.* What high school will you go to in the fall? P-town or Nauset?"

"I didn't know there was a choice," I said.

"Yeah, there's a choice for Truro kids. Razzle busses up to Nauset, but me and Primo go to P-town High. It's more fun there."

"How come you go to Nauset?" I asked Razzle.

"Because Harley goes to P-town," she said. It wasn't a joke.

"Hey, cut it out, you two," Primo said. "They're both good schools, Ken."

"I guess I'll have to figure it out over the summer."

"We'll help you figure it out," Harley said with a lovely smile. Whoa. An honest to God smile from a girl like that. I was too discombobulated to say anything, so I just flicked my tongue over my cone and splashed chocolate ice cream on my shirt in a very cool, casual way.

"See you later," Razzle said as she turned and walked away. It almost seemed as if she were dismissing me, too, but I didn't feel right staying there with Harley and Primo, who were probably a couple. I said good-bye to them and followed Razzle back out into the light.

She was sitting on the sandy grass next to the bikes, taking big enough bites from her cone to freeze a normal brain solid.

"Why'd you leave? I thought you wanted me to meet them."

"Him, not her. She's evil."

I figured it was a jealousy thing. Obviously Razzle wasn't as good-looking as Harley—girls got all bent out of shape about stuff like that, didn't they?

"Evil?" I laughed. "That's a little harsh, isn't it?"

"You don't believe me, ask Ezra. Wait a few weeks and ask Primo. She goes through guys like a lawnmower through a garden. Leaves a lot of wreckage behind."

"Ezra used to date her?"

"She was his first girlfriend. He was sixteen and she wasn't even fourteen yet, but she knew a lot more about all of it than he did. After Harley he didn't date anybody else until this year when he met Mimi. I think he's finally over her."

"Well, I won't be dating Harley," I said.

Razzle gave a sarcastic laugh. "It's not up to you, Cool Hand Luke."

Just then the screen door of Calderone's opened, and Primo came stalking out, Harley dawdling along behind him. "Raz, my band's playing Friday night. You and Kenyon should come. We're good now."

"Yeah? Where you playing?"

"They're playing at my party," Harley said. "For my six-teenth birthday." I saw now that she was wearing clunky, red high heels with thin, white socks in them. She stood with her toes pointing inward so she resembled Dorothy from Oz, *after* she'd lost her virginity to the Tin Man.

Razzle's face turned icy. "Sorry, I wasn't invited," she said.

"It's not a big deal, Razzle. Come if you want to," Harley said, without a trace of enthusiasm. Then she turned to me. "Kenny, I'll introduce you to some kids from P-town High."

"Yeah, Ken, you should come," Primo said. "Not every-body looks like me."

I laughed. At least Primo had a sense of humor. "Where is it?"

"My house," Harley shouted as she climbed into the front seat of an old Volvo next to Primo. "Razzle knows where it is." They peeled out of the gravel drive and headed for the highway.

Razzle was busy licking the drips off the inside of her arms.

"I guess Primo's older than us, huh?"

"Just a year," she said.

"The driving year, though."

"Yeah."

"And Harley is turning sixteen."

Razzle gave an exaggerated sigh. "Yes, she's older, cooler, smarter, and so far ahead of the rest of us we might as well give up chasing after her. I know *I* have."

"Did you have a run-in with her or something?"

Razzle stood up and righted her bike. "You could say that. Yeah, I ran into her the way you run into a brick wall. She doesn't look like a brick wall—she looks like an open door—but when you get there, bam, that door is *gone.*"

We rode back toward our cottages, Razzle in the lead, as usual. I worked to catch up with her. "So what happened, anyway?"

"Kenyon, I don't want to talk about Harley, okay? She makes me want to slit my wrists. Or maybe hers."

I shut up and dropped back behind her. Slit wrists seemed like sort of an overreaction to jealousy. Or maybe she was still furious with Harley for breaking up with Ezra and hurting his feelings. Anyway, I guessed we wouldn't be going to Harley's house Friday night. Of course, I could go by myself if I could find out where she lived. I didn't think I'd ask Razzle for directions, though.

She pulled her bike up just outside Mockingbird. "Here's your nest, Big Bird."

Just then my mother came around the corner; she must have been in my place. "I was looking for you, Ken. Dad said you'd gone for ice cream, but that was an hour ago." She forced herself to move her eyes over to Razzle. "Hello again."

"Hiya."

"Dad said I was done working for the day."

"You are. I just wondered when you'd be back."

She just wondered how much time I was spending with Razzle. She just wanted to make sure Razzle wasn't in the cabin with me. I guess by the time you're old enough to be a parent you forget how to be sneaky.

Razzle was staring at my mother's bare feet. I noticed it because I was too. I couldn't remember the last time I'd seen her walking around outside without shoes on. Maybe she was beginning to relax into Cape Cod.

"You've got big feet, don't you?" Razzle said. Then before

my flummoxed mother could think how to answer that, she said, "I do too. Did you know Marilyn Monroe had six toes on each foot?"

"Really?" I said.

She nodded. My mother was still looking down at her own normally toed feet.

"I better go. I'll be here tomorrow at three-thirty so we can start shooting. Should I bring along some clothes from the Swap Shop? I'll see if there are any good costumey things."

And then she was off, flying down the road on her dump bike. My mother had her mouth open, but there must have been too many complaint options for her to pick just one. Finally she closed her mouth, shook her head, and left me standing in the sand wondering how on earth I'd managed to meet so many odd people in such a small town in such a short period of time.

eight

Dad okayed my new hours—since Frank usually arrived early anyway—but then I wasn't sure I wanted him to. It occurred to me that I may have locked myself into spending all my late afternoons with Razzle, which wasn't what I had planned for the summer. On the other hand, my so-called plans primarily involved wandering around the dunes with a camera in my hands, so maybe having somebody to wander around *with* wasn't such a terrible idea.

Mom said nothing about my new schedule, or about Razzle either. Silent disapproval was her weapon of choice and it had served her well in the past, but for some reason, I felt more able to withstand the frosty looks these days.

Razzle showed up the next afternoon at three-thirty on the dot, a garbage bag full of goofy outfits strapped to her bike basket with clothesline. She was off the bike before it had stopped rolling. She waved and yelled hello to Frank, then pounced on me. "Wait till you see what I've got! Are you done painting? God, I practically got run down on Route 6—the traffic stinks already and it isn't even the Fourth of July yet. Where can I change? In your cabin?"

She was wired and about to burst with impatience, so I told her to go change her clothes in Mockingbird while

I cleaned up my painting mess. "I hope you're not going to dress like a clown or anything," I told her.

"Don't worry. You'll like it."

I was finishing folding up newspapers and washing out brushes when I saw her, already dressed, talking to Frank outside of Egret. He'd gotten ahead of me today, but I was finally done with Sandpiper now, and he was bogged down with Egret's rusted pipes, so I'd catch up to him by tomorrow morning.

The outfit she'd chosen was odd—a white filmy thing, yellowed with age at the hem and neckline, that billowed out around her knees. It might have been a fancy nightgown, or some fat woman's slip—I couldn't tell—but I suspected it would photograph nicely. I liked the way Razzle was standing now, looking Frank right in the face, dead on. Most people don't do that, and I wished I had my camera in hand already. But this shot I'd miss.

"Frank likes it!" she yelled as I approached. "He says it was probably his grandmother's!"

"I did not. I said she used to wear stuff like that. Floaty nightgowns, always white. She liked to imagine she was a Hollywood starlet," Frank said, smiling.

Razzle stood on tiptoe, her arms and face raised dramatically to the sky. "I imagine I'm a goddess!"

Frank looked at her seriously. "Now that I think of it, you do look like . . . my ninety-two-year-old grandmother."

Razzle swatted him, and he backed up just enough to avoid it. She chased him in a circle, pouting and laughing. You'd have thought they'd known each other for years.

"Enough kiddo! I'm on the job here. I gotta make a living," Frank said, holding up his hands. Razzle gave his hands a playful slap and then stopped.

"Go get the camera, Photo Boy!" she commanded.

When I stepped into Mockingbird to get my Nikon—the best Christmas gift I'd ever gotten—I noticed the garbage bag had been emptied on the bed and the various costumes laid out so I could see them, scarves and hats placed with the dresses they might accompany. It looked like half a dozen invisible women were lounging across my bedspread. Razzle's own clothes, another set of raggedy shorts and tank top, were folded neatly on the chair, her sandals resting on top of the pile.

I put a few rolls of black-and-white film in my camera bag along with the secondhand lenses I'd managed to scrape up since Christmas. It made me feel like a pro to gather all my equipment together. Before I left I took one more look at the make-believe ladies—for some reason they made me kind of sad. They were like dolls who couldn't move unless Razzle put them on and brought them to life. Man, just being around this girl made me weird. Now I was feeling sorry for *clothes.*

"Where do you want me first?" She was twisting the sand under her feet into long, narrow ditches.

I'd been thinking about it. "Maybe up against one of the cottages so the row of them show behind you," I said. "I like seeing all the identical houses growing smaller and smaller in the distance."

Frank was taking a coffee break at one of the picnic tables. "Am I in your way here?"

"Nope. I'm shooting the other direction."

The wind was just about perfect for catching the light skirt fabric and twisting it just a bit around her legs, then blowing it out to the side. I leaned her against Loon, which I thought was the most appropriate cabin, and told her to look out at the ocean, not at the camera. She put one foot up against the cottage, and the angle of her knee echoed the angle of her nose in profile. With her shadow streaming up the sand behind her, it was a great shot.

But just as I was about to take it, she straightened up and started talking again. "Oh, I forgot to tell you, Rusty's coming! On Thursday. Billie gave in. Wait till you meet her— you'll probably want to take *her* picture!"

"Uhuh. But at the moment, I'm trying to take yours. And you're *moving*. Especially your mouth."

"Sorry. I was afraid I'd forget to tell you." She went back into her pose.

"Look farther to the left."

"You won't be able to see my face."

"Razzle!" She turned left, a slight look of annoyance on her face. I took about a dozen shots of her like that, moving in and out, from different angles. I had a feeling they'd be good.

"You want me to change clothes now? Or maybe get a hat?"

Frank walked over to us. "I didn't mean to eavesdrop, but I heard you mention Rusty. I used to know somebody named Rusty, and I wondered . . ."

"Yeah, she's about your age probably," Razzle said. "Rusty Penney. She used to have real long, black hair, but now it's cut short."

"Sounds like her. How do you know her?"

Razzle gave a snicker. "I don't really know her that well. She's my mother."

Now Frank leaned back against Loon. "You're Rusty's . . .

daughter. And Billie is your grandmother. And you have a brother named Ezra."

"Yeah! How do you know all that?"

Frank was staring at Razzle. "I knew your mother a long time ago. A very long time ago."

"I'm surprised Rusty hung around with a guy who wouldn't sleep with her. No offense," Razzle said.

Frank had a *gone* look in his eyes, like he was remembering that long-ago time. "She used to date a friend of mine."

"Well, she'll be here on Thursday if you want to see her. I don't know how long she's staying this time—sometimes she only stays a night, and sometimes she stays as long as Billie'll put up with her."

Frank was staring at the wall of the cabin as if there was a movie being projected on it. It seemed to me a load of memories must be catching up to him.

"Yoo-hoo? Are you in there?" Razzle waved her hand in front of Frank's eyes. "How well did you know Rusty anyway?" She narrowed her eyes and tried to look inside him.

Frank pulled himself together and smiled at her. "Oh, not that well, really. You look like her. But you look more like . . . like yourself."

"That's what everybody says. I'm an *original*. Which means I'm not as gorgeous as she is." She shrugged. "I'm smarter, though. I don't do anything that would make Billie mad enough to kick me out of her house."

"You're plenty gorgeous, Razzle," Frank said.

"Yeah, you just think so because you're gay and I look like a boy."

Frank shook his head. "Always a wise answer. I better get back to work here and quit my daydreaming."

"I'll tell Rusty you remembered her."

Frank turned away. "She won't be surprised." His usual energetic stride seemed slower now, tired.

When he was gone Razzle turned her attention back to me. "Okay, let's do more pictures. What next?"

"That was sort of weird, don't you think?" I asked her.

"Not particularly. Rusty had a reputation."

I pressed her. "Yeah, but Frank seemed so *shocked.*"

"Rusty's pretty shocking. Wait'll you meet her."

"Razzle, you *do* know who your father is, don't you?"

"What difference does it make?"

"You *don't?*"

"He's gone! He left! Billie says he was just like Grandpa Jacob, a wanderer. She says he'll never be back, and I shouldn't think about it or hope for it."

"But Frank might know him, or at least know who he is."

She shrugged. "Maybe, maybe not."

"Aren't you even curious about it?"

"I don't *need* to know that kind of thing, Kenyon. I don't *want* to know!"

"Why not?"

She was quiet a minute, looking at her fingernails, and then she looked up and smiled. "Because I'm Raziel, the Angel of Mysteries! I'm gonna get a hat. And then let's go closer to the water, huh? I always like backlit portraits where the woman's hair is all flying, and it looks like there's a halo around it."

"You don't have enough hair for that."

"That's why I'm getting a hat," she said and marched back inside to choose her next disguise.

Okay, so I'm Kenyon, the Angel of Curiosity, but if I didn't know who my father was, and it seemed like somebody else might, I'd sure as hell ask him. Why was Razzle so brain-washed by everything Billie said? The way Frank acted, I wouldn't be surprised if Razzle's father still lived around here. Maybe he doesn't even know he *has* a daughter. Maybe Billie doesn't want her to meet her father because then she'd go off with him and leave Billie alone with nothing but a dozen dogs for company. I decided, even if Razzle didn't want to know, I'd try to find out something from Frank. Even the Angel of Mysteries might want to know who her father was sooner or later.

It was so great to be looking through the camera lens again, framing life so it looked the way I wanted it to. Razzle was a good model because she wasn't self-conscious, she didn't *fuss.* Her swingy, gawky walk looked sort of graceful in the sand, and I got nice shots of her with some stray mutt following at her heels. We took photographs for more than an hour. Neither of us brought up the subject of her father again, and Frank left while we were farther down the beach. I didn't only photograph Razzle; I did some landscapes, too, and got some nice shots of two kids pushing each other off small, flat rocks.

At five o'clock we returned to Mockingbird. Razzle changed back into Cinderella, the dump girl, and bundled her outfits into the trash bag again. "I'll keep these at home for a while, in case we need them," she said.

"You wanna go get an ice cream before you go home?" I said.

"Can't. Too late. I told Billie I'd make her a meatloaf for dinner tonight."

"Can't she cook?"

"Course she can cook, but she doesn't like to. So I do.

Besides, you just want to go back to Calderone's to see if Harley's there."

I could feel my cheeks glowing. "You're the one who introduced me to those people. Now you don't want me to speak to them?"

"Hey, you do whatever you want, Kenyon," she said, and pedaled away. She'd only gone half a block before she turned and circled back to me. "I can't meet you tomorrow—we have to get ready for Rusty—but the next day you can come up to Billie's when you're done working. Lots of good photo ops up there."

Almost immediately I began to imagine the pictures I'd take at Billie's—the herd of dogs, the overcrowded but serene living room, the Christmas lights over the sink, maybe even the playhouse in the rosebushes. But I had a feeling the real reason we were moving our operations up to Billie's house was because Razzle had been more freaked out by Frank than she'd admit.

And the really weird thing was, I was kind of sorry I couldn't see her tomorrow.

nine

Frank hadn't finished working on the kitchen sink in Egret yet, so the next morning I set up my painting gear in there. I did the cabinets first so I'd be out of his way and on to the walls by the time he arrived. This courtesy, however, wasn't enough to thrill him.

"Pugh!" He wrinkled up his face. "Why'd you have to start in here? It's bad enough to work with that paint stink in the next room—now I've got it on top of me." The morning was chilly, but he stripped down to his usual tank top once he was inside.

It's funny. It was the tank top that always reminded me Frank was gay. I guess because of what Razzle said about his muscles. And I admit there was usually a second or two, when he'd first unzip his sweatshirt, that I'd feel sort of strange. Like I shouldn't look at him too much or he'd think I was . . . I don't know . . . it's dumb, but it's hard to stop your brain thinking those things.

On the other hand, Frank was a very easy guy to hang out with. He told me great stories about P-town and about working on his dad's boat. Sometimes he'd turn up the radio station, and we'd both screech along with some cheesy eighties punk song. We both liked exactly the same kind of pizza—caramelized onions, sausage, double mozzarella—and he'd seen *Night of the Living Dead* fourteen times. He could have been my best friend except, of course, he was a thirty-five-year-old gay plumber. Just my luck.

"You'll get used to the smell in a minute," I said. "It'll be easier for us to talk if I'm in here."

Frank gave me a suspicious look. "Whata you want to talk about?"

I shrugged. "Whatever."

"If you're planning to pump me for information about how I know Razzle's mother, you can forget about it. I'm not talking." He put his stuff down and got out the wrenches he needed, then crawled underneath the sink.

I let that go, thought about my approach a little bit, then finally asked, very innocently, "Why? Is it a big secret or something?"

Frank sighed. "I don't know, is it? If it is, she's not going to find out anything from me."

I tried again. "Razzle doesn't even know who her father is. Billie just told her he left and won't be coming back."

Frank was silent for a minute. "That's true," he said finally.

"So," I pushed, "you *do* know who he is?"

"I told you, Ken, I'm not discussing this with you."

Which seemed like an admission to me. "Does he know he's got a kid? Don't you think Razzle ought to know if he knows? Why can't she know?"

Frank crawled out from under the sink, his face flushed. "Look, Ken, I'm not the person in charge of what Razzle does or doesn't know, or should or shouldn't know. If you keep pestering me about it, I'll go on to the next cabin and finish this one up later."

Why was he so upset? Razzle wasn't *his* daughter—he was gay. But I didn't like him being angry with me, so I shut up about it.

But before he crawled back under the sink, he asked me, "Does Razzle *want* to know about her father?"

"Not really," I admitted. "Seems like she's scared to find out."

"Billie could put the fear in anybody." He shook his head.

"But she might want to know sometime," I argued. "I mean, *shouldn't* she know? If other people know?"

He grimaced. "Maybe. But it's not my place to tell her, and it's not yours either."

"Okay," I agreed. We worked in silence for a long time—the white paint covering up the dirty gray like a clean sheet—until Frank got the new piece of pipe installed and crawled out again.

"Coffee break. If we don't get some fresh air soon your mom'll find our asphyxiated bodies in here at lunchtime." He gave me an elbow in the ribs so I'd know he wasn't mad anymore.

I'd found an old flat board in the cellar at the big house to set my enlarger on. It didn't take long to put everything in place and fill the trays in the bathtub with chemicals. My darkroom was ready to go.

There were two rolls of film to develop from the day before with Razzle. I did the contact sheet first, so I could see what pictures were good enough to print. A lot of them looked good. Several from the series where she was leaning against Loon seemed to be great, and a few later shots down on the beach were good too. One of the photos of the boys on the rocks was also a keeper.

I was so excited—I hadn't been able to use a darkroom since school ended in early June, and I'd never had a place to set up my own enlarger semipermanently like this. The first shot I printed was of Razzle and the stray dog on the beach. She was in profile, her weight on one leg, her arms waving in the air, the floaty dress blowing around her knees. The dog was on its back legs, its front paws paddling toward his new friend, almost as if they were dancing. I enlarged the photo so you could see the crazy look on the dog's face, as if it wanted to leap into Razzle's arms.

The best thing about developing your own pictures is putting the paper in the chemical bath and watching as the image begins to appear on the blank page. It's the closest thing to real magic I know. As the pictures began to emerge, I felt suddenly calm. I was in control of my world in the darkroom. The decisions were all mine, and so were the results.

I had no idea it was already dinnertime when I heard Mom come into the cabin. "Ken, are you coming up to our house to eat?"

When she called it "our house" like that, it always seemed to me she meant hers and Dad's. That I wasn't part of the "our" that lived there. Of course, I *wasn't* living there for the summer, and I was thrilled not to be, but still, it made me feel like the bird that got shoved out of its nest before it could actually fly. "I'm in the middle of printing. I'll make myself a sandwich later," I told her.

"Are you sure? We're having shrimp tonight."

"That's okay. Next time." I loved shrimp, but eating just couldn't compare to the excitement of the darkroom.

"How about if I bring down a plate of shrimp salad and leave it in your refrigerator?"

"Great. Thanks, Mom." Now go! I wanted to say, but, of course, I couldn't. I liked being left alone in silence when I printed, so my own thoughts could get big enough to fill the whole room. I loved the way an emerging picture sometimes startled me, the camera capturing something I hadn't seen in life. Sometimes I thought I must be blind when I wasn't looking through that Nikon.

That's how I felt printing the pictures of Razzle in the white dress. The angles were beautiful, as I'd thought, but there was more there too. The whole composition was dramatic. You felt her waiting for something. Waiting patiently, which was funny because Razzle wasn't the patient type. But there it was—in the way she leaned against the cabin and gazed at the water, in the looseness of her spine, the billowing skirt, the shadow on the sand. I'd never even seen this Razzle before. Almost . . . *quiet*.

I'd seen some of the other Razzles, though. The one that stared straight into the camera, a big, black hat tipped to one side, her eyes held wide open—I knew her—the scary Razzle, the one who called all the shots.

And the goofy Razzle was there too, with her long toes pointing toward each other and one bony hip stuck out to the side, not sure if she should go for sexy or obstinate. It turned out Razzle was a fabulous model. She changed so much from one picture to the next that you felt you were seeing many different girls instead of just one very puzzling girl. I knew immediately what I would call this series: *The Angel of Mysteries.*

When I'd finished the prints, I hung them to dry on a clothesline strung along the shower rail and then over to the blocked window. I couldn't print more than a dozen shots at a time because there was no place to dry more than that, but I was satisfied with my day's work. I carried Mom's shrimp salad outside to the picnic table so I could watch the sun set while I ate.

"There you are! Haven't seen you in days!" It was Mrs. Thackery, dressed in a long black dress with a bright purple scarf tied at her waist and several long strands of beads twirled around her neck. She'd clipped some rhinestone butterflies into her wild, white hair. I was happy to see her again.

"Hi, Mrs. Thackery. You're all dressed up. Are you going somewhere?"

"Thank you for noticing, Kenyon! I'm going to a party with an old friend this evening. Eddie Bacheldor—he's a sculptor. Perhaps you've heard of him?"

"No, I don't think . . . oh, wait . . . does he sculpt things out of used metal?" I remembered my first day at the dump when the old artist guy came in looking for scrap metal. Hadn't his name been . . . ?

"That's Eddie! We've known each other since we were young. We both lived out here for years when we were with our first spouses." She smiled at the past. "Wonderful, crazy times."

I looked at Mrs. Thackery again. My first impression of her had been totally off the mark. I'd figured she was just another old lady, but what did that mean? What if people thought of me as "just another teenager"? As though we were all alike? Mrs. Thackery was certainly not like any other old woman I'd ever met.

"Will all the people at the party be artists?" I asked.

"Well, most of them were at one time or another," she said. "Some gave it up and got jobs where they could actually earn a living." She laughed. "Only the most foolish of us still do it."

Suddenly I wanted her to see my pictures. "Do you have five minutes?" I asked. "I've just printed some photographs in my darkroom. I'd like you to see them."

"Oh, it would be a privilege!" she said. "I can listen for Eddie's foggy old car horn from your cabin."

The pictures were dry enough by then to bring out into the kitchen and lay on the counter so she could see them better. For a few minutes she just looked, not saying anything, picking up one and then another, as if she was studying them. I was starting to worry that she hated them, but at least I knew she was really looking at them, not like the people who glance at your work and then toss off a quick remark like, "Wow! Great! Now can we go?"

Finally Mrs. Thackery looked up at me, no smile on her face. "Kenyon, you are a remarkable photographer for such a young man. I wasn't expecting work like this from a boy." My heart started thrumming loudly. Yes! I knew they were good!

She picked up two photos of Razzle, one in the white dress and one of the close-ups with the black hat. "These are startling. You must know this girl very well. Is she your muse?"

I stuttered. "Well, no, I mean, she's sort of a friend, but . . . I don't actually know her that well . . . my muse?"

"I say that because of the strength of the photos. I feel I know who she is, just looking at them, so I imagine you must know her well too. Or perhaps it's just that she knows herself." Mrs. Thackery touched the edges of the photo she was holding as though she were caressing Razzle's face.

Just then we heard the horn, tooting a few cabins down the

line, at Shearwater. Mrs. Thackery looked a little disappointed. "Oh, dear. Will you invite me back again sometime to see more of your photographs?"

"Sure, Mrs. Thackery. Any time."

She took up her small silk purse and said, "No more Mrs. Thackery, though. It makes me feel ancient. Besides, we're friends now. Call me Lydia, please."

"Okay, Lydia."

She smiled at me, then took a little jump through my doorway. I could hear her calling to Eddie Bacheldor as she hurried down the road toward his car. "Prompt as ever, Eddie. You never change!"

Frank wasn't around much of the day on Thursday—he had to go up to Hyannis to get some parts for the old tub in Egret—and I was impatient to get done with my lonely painting job and get over to Razzle's house. Or rather, Billie's house. I'd noticed that everybody called it that, even Ezra, which seemed sort of odd. They'd all lived there forever, hadn't they? And yet they didn't seem to claim any rights to it. It was always "Billie's house."

I wanted to show Razzle the photos, and I also wanted to take more pictures of her up there, in her own exotic surroundings. And then there was Rusty to meet. It promised to be an interesting day.

I was pedaling down 6A when I noticed two familiar figures up ahead, one slouched in a crooked wooden booth by the roadside, the other outside the booth, leaning into it. I recognized Primo by his hair and Harley by the graceful way she waved her butt around just enough to stop traffic. My God.

"Hey!" I called to them as I pulled up. Harley looked at the bike first, ran her dark eyes lightly over my skinny body, and turned her back on me. This was the kind of reception I was used to from pretty girls—they couldn't *see* me, or maybe they just wouldn't look. If you'd asked a girl at Hancock if she knew me she'd probably say, "I think so. Is he tall? I don't really know him." And they didn't. My Invisible Man routine had worked a little too well. It seemed like it might be time to morph back into a tangible person, if only I knew how.

Primo's memory was better than Harley's. "Yo! Razzle's friend. Kenyon, right?" He sat up a little straighter in his wooden cage. "How's it goin'?"

Harley gave me a second glance and rearranged her mouth into a slick smile. "Oh, right! I didn't recognize you. Is that your brother's bike?"

"I don't have a brother. I'm just using this until I can get my license."

She nodded knowingly. "I'm getting mine next week. Until then I just use Primo," she said, leaning over and nuzzling his ear to show she was joking. Or maybe just to show me she was taken—I wasn't sure which. I didn't need a reminder; I knew a girl like Harley would never be interested in a guy like me.

"What are you guys doing here?" I asked.

"This is my summer job, if you can believe it," Primo said. "The pay sucks, but it's the easiest job on the lower Cape." He pointed to a painted sign over the booth that I hadn't even noticed. MILTON'S DUNE BUGGY TOURS. $20 PER PERSON PER HOUR.

"You sell tickets?"

"Now and then. The rest of the time I sit here and

sunbathe. Sometimes I bring my acoustic guitar along to practice."

"The buggies leave from over there," Harley said, nodding her head toward a tumbling-down garage just across the dune. "Billie drives for Milton most days. She's off today, though. You know who Billie is, doncha?"

"Yeah. Razzle's grandma. I've met her."

Harley grinned. "Are you and Weird Wanda a *thing?*"

"God, Harley, the way you talk about people!" Primo looked at me. "Razzle's a good kid, really. She's just a little strange is all."

"She's not my girlfriend or anything, if that's what you mean," I said. "She was the first person I met when I moved here, and she's sort of been showing me around."

Harley laughed. "Well, that's a short tour, since Razzle never goes anyplace but the dump."

"I don't know why you don't like her, Harley. What did she ever do to you?" Primo asked.

"She *lived.*" Harley sighed. "Okay, I'm sorry I'm being so mean. It's just that I'm sick of this stupid town and all the same stupid people that show up here every damn summer. And it's only the end of June. I don't think I'm gonna make it, Primo. I have to get *out* of here!"

Primo didn't respond to her pretty complaints. "So, Ken, what are you doing this summer? You got a job?"

"I work for my parents," I admitted. "Painting. They just bought the old Landmark Cottages down the road, and we're fixing up the cabins and then renting them out."

"*Really?*" Harley stared at me in wondrous disbelief I couldn't interpret.

"Really. Why is that so startling?"

"She's looking for a chambermaid job," Primo explained. "A Saturday turnover thing. And most of the cottage colonies already have their staff."

"Tell me your parents haven't hired anybody yet!" Harley begged, her eyes closed, her lips pursed, her hand squeezing off the blood supply in my wrist.

"I don't think so. This is the first week we've had guests. My mother's been doing the cleaning herself, but once we get more cabins open she'll probably need help."

"Primo, take me right now!" she ordered, giving him a little shove.

"I can't! I'm working!"

"You're not *doing* anything."

"So? It's my job to not do anything."

"It's only a couple of blocks from here," I said. "You can walk."

"I'll be sweaty by the time I get there!" she said, still looking pleadingly at Primo.

"Chambermaids are supposed to be sweaty," he said. "Yes, you look adorable when you're begging, but I'm not gonna get my ass fired from the best job I ever had just so *you* can get a job."

"Fine," she said, suddenly self-reliant in her annoyance. "I'll see you later then." As she brushed past me, she put her hand around the back of my neck, which immediately raised goosebumps all down my back. "Thanks for the tip, Ken. If I get the job I'll be seeing you all the time, huh? Wouldn't Razzle love *that?*" She laughed and began to sizzle her way down Route 6A.

I guess Primo noticed me noticing her. "She's somethin' else, isn't she?" he said.

"Sorry," I said.

"Hey, I don't own her. Nobody owns Harley. This is my second go-round, so I know what to expect. Which is, nothin'. This time I'm just trying not to get too attached."

"That must be hard."

"Yeah, it is." He laughed. "Just ask any guy in town."

ten

I could hear the yelling before I got to the end of the wooden path and dropped my bike in the sand. Parked next to Ezra's truck and Billie's Jeep was an ancient, rusted Toyota that looked like it hadn't had a bath in decades. Its owner, I supposed, was one of the noisemakers. I probably would have turned around and gotten the hell out of there right then except that Razzle, who was outside on the porch surrounded by dogs, saw me, and then so did the pooches.

It's the commotion they make as they come galloping at you that's frightening, but if you keep your eyes open you can see that all twelve tails are wagging. I picked up Betsy-Wetsy and let her smooch my face, and the other eleven trailed along beside me as I crossed the yard to where Razzle sat on an old rocking chair.

"Hey, you came," she said, seemingly oblivious to the ruckus going on inside.

"Maybe I should leave, huh?" I glanced toward the house.

She shook her head. "Nah. This is how it always is when Rusty shows up. You wanna go meet her?"

"Doesn't sound like this is a good time."

"There might not be a good time, Kenyon. Believe me."

She got up and started toward the door. "Better leave Betsy outside. Rusty's allergic."

Allergic? How could anybody who was allergic spend five minutes here?

Billie was standing tall in front of the Jim Morrison flag, pointing across the room at a small woman dressed all in black whose enormous dark eyes sent lightning flashes back.

"I knew it would be bad when I did my cards this morning," Billie trumpeted. "The Empress is always trouble for me—it means everything is out of control!"

"If you're going to do tarot, at least get the symbols right," Rusty spit back. "The Empress means passion and emotion—two things you never really understood."

"Don't you tell me how to read my cards! You don't even believe in the cards—you believe a bunch of stupid angels are leading you around by the nose!"

"You have no idea what I believe, Billie!"

"And vice versa!" Billie shot back.

Ezra came out of a back room dragging a sleeping bag. "Would you two shut the hell up? It's bad enough I have to sleep on the couch for God knows how long. Do I have to listen to this bullshit besides?" He threw the bag on the couch and went back into his room.

"I'm sorry, Ez," Rusty called in. She seemed a little unsteady on her legs as she walked to his doorway. "You know I have to be able to shut the door on those damn dogs." To emphasize her point, she gave a dainty sneeze. "If Billie didn't live in a friggin' *kennel* . . ."

"I'll live my life any way I damn . . ."

"HEY!" Razzle yelled. "We've got a guest!"

Never have I felt more like an intruder. Billie and Rusty

both turned to look at me, their eyes blinking in confusion at finding a stranger entering the ring.

"Billie, you remember Kenyon," Razzle said. Billie stared at me.

Ezra came out of the back room again, carrying a stack of clothes that he piled on top of a small TV set. He rocked back a little when he noticed me, but grinned. "Welcome to the Fight Club. Have you met our charming mother yet?"

Rusty had a smirk on her face by this time. "You mean you're actually lettin' me meet one a' your friends, Raz?" she asked as she carefully picked her way over to me. Her path was blocked by an enormous chew toy that she kicked into a precariously stacked pile of books. The kick unbalanced her a little, and she steadied herself on the back of a chair as she held out her hand.

"I'm Rusty," she said, lowering her heavily fringed eyelids before peering up into my face. Billie might not win the prize for Most Likely to Be a Grandmother, but never had I imagined a mother like Rusty existed. For some reason a saying my grandmother used to use suddenly came to mind: *It looks like she was rode hard and put up wet.* It referred, of course, to horses, but after taking Rusty's cold, shaky hand in mine, and watching the little drops of sweat bead up on the cakey makeup under her nose, I knew I'd never hear it again without thinking of her.

"This is my friend, Kenyon," Razzle told her.

"*Kenyon.* What a name," she said, breathing in my face.

"Nice to meet you."

"He's a photographer," Razzle continued. "He's been taking pictures of me."

"With your clothes off?" Rusty asked easily.

Ezra groaned and went back into his room. Billie came to life again. "With her *clothes* off? Are you out of your mind? Well, I know you're out of your mind—why am I askin' that?"

"Just regular photographs, Rusty," Razzle explained. "Not porn or anything."

Rusty looked disgusted. "I didn't mean *porn*. Is that the kind of thing Billie teaches you? A nude body isn't automatically porn, Razzle. It's a beautiful thing. You shouldn't be ashamed of your body."

"I'm not," Razzle said, crossing her arms across her chest, but Rusty wasn't listening.

"Artists, you know, have always celebrated nudity."

"Oh, well, then, by all means, let's *us* celebrate nudity too," Billie said, throwing her arms up into the air. "Let's throw a party for nudity. Let's get some of those beautiful artists up here and all get naked. Grownups, children, everybody!" Billie stomped into the kitchen. "For Chrissakes, all I needed was another fruitcake in this house." She plunged her hands into a sink filled halfway up with clams and water.

"Maybe we should go outside for a while," I dared to say.

"There's a kid with a brain," Billie said. "And the resta yuz shut the hell up while I clean my clams. Took me all morning to dig these beauties; I'm not gonna let 'em go to waste just because you wanna argue."

"*I* wanna argue?"

Razzle followed me out the door and around to the front of the house where we couldn't hear so much of it. "So, whataya think?" she said.

"Of what?"

"Rusty. She's a kick in the head, isn't she?"

I leaned down to pet Randolph, who'd trotted over. How was I supposed to answer that? Never had I seen a family go after each other like that. Certainly not my family—not any family I'd ever known. But Razzle seemed almost proud to live here in the midst of the battleground.

"She's something," I said. "She seemed like she might have been a little . . ." I hesitated to say it.

"Drunk? Yeah, she usually is. You don't always notice it so much. I guess she must have liquored up pretty good so she could stand seeing Billie again."

We started walking in the direction of the playhouse. "Why do they hate each other so much?" I asked. "I mean, they're mother and daughter!"

Razzle straightened her spine. "That's just biology, Kenyon. You don't get to choose who your mother is, do you? Or your kid, either."

"I know, but . . . didn't they ever get along?"

"Not since I've been here. I think it started when Rusty was such a wild teenager. Funny thing is, people say Billie was wild when she was a kid too. I think she didn't want Rusty goin' off and gettin' pregnant so young, like she did herself. And then when Rusty turned out to be even *worse* than Billie, that was the end of it."

"So Rusty just moved away."

"Yup."

"And you and Ezra stayed with Billie." I didn't say it like a question, but I wondered why.

"Rusty couldn't take care of us. She moves around all the time, all kinds of weird jobs. She's had about seven thousand boyfriends. I like her all right, but I'd rather live with Billie." Razzle made a face and studied her short fingernails. "I always think it'll be more fun to have her here than it really is. I mean, it's not boring with Rusty around, but she gets on everybody's nerves in about five minutes. Especially Billie's."

"Why does she even come back if she and Billie hate each other so much? You and Ezra could go visit her."

She sighed. "Costs too much. Anyway, I don't like to leave the Cape. I like it here." She sped up as we neared the play-house. "Come see my place. It's all fixed up."

I could see she'd done a good deal of work on it, propping up the sides with scrap wood and tying the back edges into the bushes to stabilize it. She'd even rigged up a tarp over the top to keep out the weather.

But one more question scratched at my mind. "You *have* left the Cape before, though, haven't you? I mean, for a trip or something?"

She smiled. "Nope. Never did."

"*Never?* You've never once been off this sixty-mile-long peninsula? In your whole life?"

"Nope."

"Not even to go up to Boston?"

She shook her head. "Our class took a field trip there once in seventh grade, but I didn't go. You didn't have to."

"But why not? There's a whole big world out there!"

"There's a whole big world here," she said. "Most Cape people don't like to leave if they don't have to." She motioned me to follow her inside the small house.

I had to crawl to get in, then sit cross-legged in one corner in order for there to be room for Razzle, too. Not because the area was so small, but because most of it was taken up by junk, odd stuff: a blender, an iron, an old TV set with all the knobs broken off, a mop head, some shoes, mismatched dishes and silverware. It was a mini-dump she'd created for herself out here.

"What's all the stuff for?"

"I'm making things out of it," she said.

"What kind of things?"

"Can't tell yet. It's a secret. I want to make something to show at the Dump Dance and Art Show at the end of the summer."

"What's a dump dance?"

She threw her head back, and it bumped a vacuum cleaner handle. "The Dump Dance is this great event—with a band and a bonfire and lots of food—it's our way of saying good-bye to summer and to the tourists and everything. And last year we started having an art show to go along with it, because so many dump people are also artists. This year I want to be in the art show."

I glanced at the paraphernalia she'd collected. "What kind of art do you make out of a blender and a mop?"

"I'm still at the thinking stage." She narrowed her eyes at me. "You're not the only creative person, you know."

"Me? Creative? I thought I was a Perwim."

She ignored the question, leaned forward, and poked her finger into my chest. "*You* should be in the art show. With your pictures!"

Which reminded me that I'd brought along the shots I'd taken earlier in the week. I got them out of my backpack and passed them over to her.

"I think those top ones are the best," I said. "Mrs. Thackery, or rather, Lydia, this artist who's been at the Birdhouses, really liked them too. You think they're good enough for the dump art show?"

Razzle was staring at the photos. "Wow. These are me? God, nobody ever took pictures like this of *me*. These are wonderful."

"Thanks."

"Would you really put me in the art show? I mean, my pictures?"

"Sure, if I can. I think they turned out pretty good."

She held up a photo of her in the white dress, one of the ones in which she seems so quiet. "Do I really look like this?"

I laughed. "Well, it's you, isn't it?"

"I don't know," she said, looking at it again. I took my camera from the backpack and snapped a few close-up shots of Razzle staring at herself. These would have a much different feel to them, the low light in the playhouse, the busy, crowded background, but I liked getting shots of her here, where she seemed so comfortable.

"Hold that one up again," I directed.

She held it right under her chin, her impish face shading the angel. Good one.

"By the way, I'm calling the series of white dress pictures, *The Angel of Mysteries,*" I said, thinking she'd love the idea.

Her grin faded, replaced by what seemed to be a trace of fear, or maybe just worry. I wondered if she thought I was kidding, making a joke at her expense. "Really," I said. "I think it's a perfect title."

"I guess," she said as she stuffed the photos back into the folder I'd brought them in and tried to change the subject.

"Tomorrow night is Harley's party," she said. She tied a ribbon around the mop head and then untied it again.

"Wait. Don't you want me to use that name?"

She shrugged. "It's okay. As long as you mean it. As long as you're not . . . making fun of it."

"I'm not!" I said.

She looked right into my eyes. The Nikon came up between us almost on its own, capturing, I hoped, the intensity of the look I couldn't meet without it. I guess what scared me was that to Razzle I was definitely not invisible. It seemed like she could see more of me than I wanted her to. More than I wanted anybody to.

"Enough pictures now!" she said, brushing the camera aside. "I'm not in the mood anymore." She leaned back and put her hands in front of her face to stop me.

"Okay. I won't take any more." She didn't move. "What were you saying before? About Harley's party." I noisily stuffed the camera in my backpack.

She kept her hands up and mumbled into them. "I said, *it's tomorrow.*"

"Oh, *right,*" I said, like it had slipped my mind.

Slowly she put her hands down, peeking first to make sure I wasn't waiting to ambush her. "I'm not going."

"You're not?"

She shook her head. "You can go if you want to. She lives back up in there," she said, pointing vaguely to the south. I wouldn't be able to find my own house with directions like that, but I couldn't imagine asking her for more explicit ones.

"If I went I wouldn't know anybody there but Primo and Harley," I said.

Razzle folded her legs underneath her and nodded. The playhouse was really not too comfortable for anyone who hadn't already become a yoga master. My calves were cramping, and my knees kept shooting off little fireworks of pain. "How come you and Harley don't like each other?" I asked as I tried to shift my weight to a tolerable position.

She thought it over for a minute while she squeezed a deflated football between her hands like an accordion. "I hate her because she's the meanest bitch that ever lived. And she hates me because I say it out loud. It killed me when she was going with Ezra because I knew she'd be ugly to him eventually—she always is—but he wouldn't believe me. He was just like all the other guys who fall over at her feet. It pissed me off Ezra would be that dumb, but then when she dumped him and he was all wrecked, I never said I-told-you-so. It wasn't really his fault. She *does* that to guys."

I nodded. "Okay, you've convinced me."

"Of what?"

"I do not want to go to that party!"

She smiled. "Good. That was my plan."

"Really? You were so subtle."

She bounced happily on her knees. "Say, have you ever been to a flea market? I mean, a really *good* flea market? With great junk?"

In two more minutes my legs would be so completely asleep Razzle would have to drag me out of here by the arms. "Probably not. I assume you have, though."

"In Wellfleet, every weekend. Billie usually sets up a table, and I help her out. You wanna come with us Saturday morning?"

"Why not? If it's the thing to do."

"We go early, though."

I groaned. "It's my day off! How early?"

"Gotta be there by eight to get the early customers."

"Couldn't we just get the late customers?"

She slapped my throbbing knee. "Look at it *this* way. You can go to bed real early tomorrow night now that you're not going to that stupid party!"

Unable to stand another second of agony, I elbowed my way out of the playhouse and lay on the ground recovering from paralysis of the lower extremities while Betsy washed my face as though it was her job. And I looked at it Razzle's way. When you were with her, it was hard not to.

eleven

I spent some time Friday night with Mrs. Thackery—Lydia—since I knew she'd be leaving the next day. She couldn't paint because the canvases wouldn't be dry by the time she had to pack them into her car, so she was doing ten-minute drawings instead. The idea, she said, was to reveal the important lines quickly, the form and design of the work, without losing the energy of it.

I let her draw me for a while—clothed, of course. I didn't care how beautiful Rusty thought nude bodies were, I wasn't revealing mine to anybody—not that Lydia asked me to. After a while she set up a still life to draw—some fruit and coffee cups next to an old toaster—so it would be easier for us to talk.

"How was the party the other night?" I asked her.

"Very nice. Many of my old friends were there—most of them just as pompous and ridiculous as they used to be." She laughed. "But when you've known people for fifty years, you overlook all that. They become your family. You have no choice but to love them—they're such a part of you."

"I guess you're good friends with Eddie?" I'd been wondering about the two of them ever since I'd watched Lydia run down the road to meet him.

She drew the bottom of the pear rounder and fatter than it really was, like the bottom of a bass violin. "Eddie and I," she said quietly, "have a complicated history."

I knew it! They'd been lovers when they were young! Lydia had probably been a beauty in those days, when her hair had color and her face wasn't so saggy. "Really?" I asked, wondering if she'd tell me the whole story.

"No, no," she said laughing. "I think you're getting the wrong idea. You see, Eddie's wife and my husband . . . well, Eddie and I were betrayed together. It's a strange thing to have in common."

I guess I looked shocked. I mean, no adult had ever told me anything like that before. I was just getting used to calling this woman by her first name—how was I supposed to respond to an announcement like this?

"Oh dear," Lydia said, smiling kindly. "That was more than you wanted to know, wasn't it? I understand—it's hard to believe that old people ever had a real life."

"No, that's not it," I said, although that was part of it. "It's hard to believe that my *parents* ever had a life, but I'm willing to believe other people might have."

That made her laugh so hard she put down her charcoal and sat on the couch. "I remember that exactly!" she said. "One's parents could never be imagined as other than their current fuddy-duddy selves. Generation to generation, that doesn't change."

I was starting to imagine her party in more detail—elderly folks in long scarves and gaudy clothes sneaking away from the crowd for secret make-out sessions. Ugh—too weird—it gave me the shivers.

"You don't have to answer this," I said, "but did your husband and Eddie's wife ever get married or anything?"

"No. They ran off to California together—David and Sophia were their names. David never came back—he died about ten years ago. But Sophia moved back here again. It's her home."

"Do you ever see her?" I knew I was being obnoxiously nosy, but I was caught up in the story now.

"Certainly! I see her every summer. She was at the party."

"She was?"

"Child, at my age, you forgive people. You don't necessarily forget, mind you, but there aren't enough friends left to spurn those who've wronged you in the past. And I have so much in common with Sophia—we loved the same man! In the end it brought us together." She smiled as she packed her charcoals back in their brown box. "Besides, if Sophia hadn't taken David away, I would never have met Lawrence, to whom I was happily married for thirty-seven years!"

I hated to say good-bye to Lydia. I'd never met anyone like her. She made you think maybe old people *were* wiser, at least a few of them. I carried her heaviest supplies out to the trunk of her car before I went back to my cabin so she wouldn't have to do it in the morning.

"No need to say good-bye—I'll be back for the end of the season," she assured me. "I wouldn't miss the Dump Dance and Art Show!"

I told her I was considering entering some of my photographs in the show.

"Absolutely! I'll look forward to it all summer. Especially more photos of your young muse."

"She isn't really my muse," I protested.

"Oh, I think she is," Lydia said, "whether you know it or not."

★ ★ ★

I staggered out of bed at seven-thirty the next morning, drank some juice, and ran up to the house for a quick shower before Razzle and Billie showed up. I was combing my hair when Mom knocked on the bathroom door.

"Are they here?" I called out.

Without any more invitation than that, she walked in. "Not yet, and neither is that girl you sent here looking for work."

"Who?"

"That girl—she's named after a motorcycle . . ."

"Harley! Did you hire her?"

"I did. She said she'd had experience, and I didn't feel like interviewing two dozen high school girls—anybody can scour a tub. But I told her to be here *by* eight o'clock. I very clearly said *by* eight, not ten minutes after."

I looked at my watch. "It's just eight now. I'm sure she'll be here." I didn't bother to tell Mom Harley had had her sixteenth-birthday party the night before. It wouldn't change her opinion anyway; being on time was her religion.

"You would think on her first day she'd want to make a good impression." Mom looked over my shoulder into the mirror, pushing her bangs out of her face. "I need a haircut."

I doubted very much that Harley cared what kind of impression she made on my mother. "She's a chambermaid, Mom, not the new chairman of the board. It's a summer job."

"That doesn't mean you don't do your best! How do you know her anyway? She introduced herself as a friend of yours, but I knew that was an exaggeration. The only person I ever see you with is that dump girl."

I let that comment go. "That's how I met her—Razzle knows her. They grew up together. . . ."

"Wonderful. A friend of *Razzle's*." She left the bathroom and I followed her.

"Actually they're not friends. . . ." I went to the window to see if Raz and Billie were there yet, but instead I saw Harley jumping out of Primo's car. Whoa. She was wearing short shorts and a tank top, the same outfit Razzle always wore, but on Harley it had an entirely different fit. "Here she is—you can stop ranting."

Mom went out to meet her and I went out too, to wait for the Jeep.

Harley gave Mom a big, phony-baloney smile and then turned around to wink at me, like we were in on some joke Mom wasn't.

"I said eight o'clock, did I not?" Mom started right in.

"Yeah, you did! And it's eight o'clock, right?"

"By my watch, it's five minutes after," Mom said, holding out her arm for Harley to see. "I would also prefer you to cover your . . . chest a little more. This is a place of business."

Harley looked stunned. "It's hot. This is what I always wear to clean."

"It's all right for today, but after this you'll wear a T-shirt." Mom strode off toward the building with the washers and dryers. Harley turned around and gave me an exasperated look, as if I'd forced her to work for this heartless ogre, then sauntered into the laundry shed to learn to fold towels Mom's way.

Billie drove like Ezra on speed. Razzle explained that we were late—Rusty's fault, though I didn't exactly understand why—and now Billie wanted to get to the flea market ten minutes ago. The top was down, and I had the feeling I was going to fly out over the windshield every time she hit a bump. And I think she was *looking* for bumps to hit.

By the time we turned into the Wellfleet Drive-In Theater the lot was already crowded with sellers setting up their areas. Some people had elaborate tables and tarpaulins while others just sold out of the backs of their cars. Billie had brought a table, which I knew because it was wedged into the backseat of the Jeep in front of my knees. It was possible the table and the three huge boxes on the seat next to me would have—in the event of an actual emergency—pinned me into the car.

"Damn it to hell," Billie said, disgustedly. "Now look. The good spots are all taken. We'll end up way in the back."

"It doesn't matter that much. People walk the whole thing," Razzle said.

"Not everybody. The tourists get tired out. They wanna go to the *beach*," she said, as though a local would never come up with such an insane idea.

I couldn't get out of the car until the boxes and table were unloaded, but then Billie put me to work unwrapping the precious items for display. As I lifted them from their protective newspaper I couldn't believe *these* were the things she hoped to sell. There were lots of glass bottles, some of them just regular blue glass Perrier bottles with the labels washed off, some of them dulled and smoothed by a long time in the ocean, but basically just your average beer receptacle. And then there was a huge pile of mismatched dishes and bowls, some of which I would bet came from the dump. There were about ten old sweaters, most of them with pill balls all over them, which Razzle folded carefully and laid out on a small blanket next to the table. Four or five picture frames, one with a terrible watercolor painting still inside it. A ceramic frog. A box of pencils that all said *Elwood Motor Lodge, 470 Old Cape Highway, Truro, Massachusetts* on them. A glass lighting fixture that was full of dead bugs. And that was about it. If somebody offered her five dollars for the whole lot, she'd be lucky. Of course there was also a sign stuck on the windshield of the Jeep announcing TAROT CARD READINGS—$25, but how many people came to a flea market to have their fortunes told?

"How much do you have to pay to rent a space here?" I asked Razzle.

"Twenty-five bucks. It's not bad."

"Twenty-five dollars?" I tried to keep my voice low so Billie couldn't hear me. "Every week? You'll never make that much on this old junk."

Razzle laughed. "Hey, Billie, Kenyon doesn't think we'll make our table price on this old junk."

Thank you, Razzle.

Billie snorted. "That's because he doesn't appreciate beauty."

"A Perwim," Razzle pronounced, shaking her head.

"He's the kind of person throws stuff like this out," Billie continued, "which is fine with me, because I'm the kind of person that goes around and picks it up."

Since Razzle was obviously no ally of mine today, I defended myself to Billie. "I just meant you'd have to sell an awful lot of this stuff to make up twenty-five dollars. How much can you sell a bottle for, anyway?" I picked up a Perrier bottle.

Billie looked at what I had in my hand. "Those there only get a buck or two, I grant ya, but those that've been in the ocean, the tourists really go for. I can get ten bucks easy for those. Sometimes more. Depends on the customer."

I was about to dispute her on this point when a couple in Bermuda shorts strolled over, their hands interlocked so tightly they looked welded together.

"Good morning," the woman sighed happily.

"'Lo there," Billie answered, then turned her back to them and lifted an eyebrow in my direction. "You folks lookin' for anything special?"

The young woman giggled, pushed her frizzy hair back out of her face, and looked into the man's eyes. He seemed a little embarrassed, but he smiled. "It's our honeymoon!" she said. I had the feeling we weren't the first people to hear that announcement this morning. "We want to find something . . . you know . . . *special*. To help us remember this week."

Billie nodded slowly, changing before my eyes from an irascible clamdigger and dune-buggy driver into a kindly Cape Cod antique seller whose joy in life was finding the perfect item a newlywed couple could treasure forever. "Lemme think about that one for a minute. Something *special* . . ."

Acting genes clearly ran in the family. "Gram?" said Razzle. "We do have that *one* special item. *You* know!"

"What?" the new bride wanted to know, her eyes wide.

"Gram" pointed to Razzle. "Maybe you're right, Honey. That might be just the thing they're lookin' for. It surely is one of a kind."

"What?" the frizzy-haired giggler demanded to know.

Billie's hand floated over the bottle selection for just a moment. "Most of these are just plain old bottles, but one a' them . . . here it is!" She pulled a weathered brown beer bottle from the pack and held it up to the sun. "See that?" she asked.

The couple stared intently at the bottle. "Is it a note?" Frizzy asked.

"That's what it is," Billie said. "Unfortunately, I've never been able to get it out to see what it says."

"Oh, I wish we knew what was on it!"

The bridegroom came to life now—getting things out was a man's job. "Have you got anything long and thin, like a chopstick, maybe?" he wanted to know once he'd assessed the situation.

"A chopstick! There's an idea. I think I do have a pair of chopsticks here *somewhere*." Amazingly, Razzle knew just where those chopsticks were. Bridegroom, meanwhile, was chewing up a piece of gum Frizzy had had in her mailbag-sized purse.

The inventor stuck the piece of gum onto the chopstick and lowered it into the bottle, while Billie, Frizzy, Razzle, and I watched, enthralled. Sure enough, he wrestled that paper out! It looked very old, all crumpled, with runny ink.

"You can still read it, though!" said Frizzy. "Oh, my God, look at this! It says *No matter how far apart we are, I will never forget you!*" She looked up at her new hubby. "Oh, Robbie, this is perfect! We have to get it!"

"Twenty-five dollars," Billie said casually. "You know, with the message and all."

I had a feeling Robbie wasn't that dumb, but hey, for twenty-five dollars they'd gotten their special thing. And it was still early. Plenty of time left to go to the beach.

As soon as they walked away Billie held the money up in front of my face. "I guess we'll make our table price after all."

Razzle got another message out of the glove box of the Jeep.

"They all say the same thing?" I asked.

"It's kind of all purpose," Razzle said.

"Don't you think there's something a little illegal about it? Or at least unethical?"

Billie pointed at me. "Hey, they want some romance— that's what I give 'em. They ain't payin' for the bottle, for Chrissakes."

She'd brought a copy of the *Utne Reader* along and climbed into the front seat of the Jeep to read while Razzle manned the table. She put on a baseball cap that said "Spiritus Pizza" and propped her feet up on the dashboard behind the tarot readings sign. Talk about an original.

"Would you mind if I took a few pictures of you?" I asked her.

"I certainly would mind," she said. "Point that thing in my direction and you won't have it much longer."

"Take me, take me!" Razzle begged. I was disappointed not to get Billie, the chameleon, in one of her disguises, but Razzle was a good subject too in rhinestone-studded sun-glasses and a leopard-skin polyester blouse—her dress-up clothes, I presumed, for the flea market. She sat on a folding chair, her elbows at the edge of the bottle-covered table. I took a few of those and then walked down the aisle a little ways, thinking maybe I could get some with Billie in the background, at least. I was nervous, though, that she'd know what I was doing, so I only took one.

"Take me close up," Razzle said, removing her sunglasses. "Take my eyes."

She had an interesting expression on her face, very serious, so I took the picture. And then, while I was still looking through the lens, I imagined there were tears running down her cheeks. I don't know why. When I put the camera down, she looked fine, but she continued to stare at me, which made me uncomfortable.

"That's enough pictures for now," I said. And when that didn't stop her: "What are you looking at?"

"You," she said softly. "Did you know that your eyes are always the same size from the day you're born, but your nose and ears keep growing forever?"

"Really?"

"Um-hmm. And a pig's orgasm lasts for thirty minutes."

My muse.

twelve

We could tell summer was in full swing by the parade of cars that now raced past Baker's Birdhouses, boogie boards strapped to their roofs. A trip to Hyannis could take more than two hours if you hit the traffic wrong, and on Saturdays, turnover day for most weekly rentals, the locals stayed off the roads as much as possible.

Mom and Dad and I went into Provincetown for dinner again, to the same little place we'd liked a few weeks before, only this time there was a line out the door and the maitre d' barked that we'd have at least a forty-five minute wait, as though he was annoyed we'd come at all. I didn't mind waiting, but standing there squashed between happy vacationers made Mom and Dad furious, and after ten minutes they couldn't take it anymore. So we drove to the Dairy Queen, waited another fifteen minutes, and ended up with mountains of onion rings and fried clams. Dad also ended up with heartburn.

I was glad I had Frank to hang around with most days—his mood was always far superior to my parents'. He even taught me a few things about plumbing once in a while—the simple stuff—clogs and snakes and washers. We didn't talk about Razzle much, although if she came by, which she sometimes did, Frank was very nice to her, in a way I knew she appreciated. He'd tease her about her short haircut, or her long fingers, or something silly like that, and she'd swat at him, almost like they were flirting . . . but *kinder* than flirting.

One day she happened to be there at lunchtime, which pissed my mother off. She brought down my usual two sandwiches, a bag of chips, and a jug of iced tea. "Sorry," she said to Razzle, though obviously she wasn't one bit sorry. "I didn't bring you anything. I thought you worked weekdays."

"I don't work on Fridays," Razzle said, not looking at her.

"Well, Kenyon *does,*" Mom said.

"I know. That's why I came at lunchtime," Razzle said. The thing about Mom and Razzle was that they both always wanted to have the last word on the subject.

"Too bad you didn't think to bring your own lunch," Mom said.

"You can have one of my sandwiches," I told Raz. "I don't need two."

"Just give me half of one," she said. "I don't get very hungry on days I don't work."

Anyway, that was the day I showed Frank and Razzle my darkroom. They were impressed. Not so much by the rigged-up tables in the sink and shower, but by the enlarger and the sequence of events that brought the photos hanging across the shower curtain to life.

"You got Billie in that picture at the flea!" Razzle shouted.

"Don't tell her—please?"

"She'd kill you if she knew. She hates having her picture taken."

"Does she think it steals her soul? That's what some people believe," I said.

"She thinks it steals her privacy."

"Billie," Frank said. He stared at the picture as if he'd seen it before.

"How do you know Billie, again?" Razzle asked, then immediately decided against the question. "I guess everybody knows Billie, don't they?"

Frank nodded. "True."

Razzle looked at him from the corners of her eyes. "You never came up to visit Rusty, didja?"

"I will, one of these days," he said. "Did you tell her you met me?"

Razzle chewed her bottom lip. "No. It's been kind of hard to talk to Rusty this time. She's been, kind of . . . not feeling too good."

Frank nodded. "Just as well I didn't come around bothering her, then."

"Yeah. She spends a lot of time resting."

You could have driven a truck through the holes in that conversation, the things the two of them weren't saying.

On July fourth we had lobsters for dinner—a rare treat even though we were now living in the Land of Lobster. Not because they were expensive, but because neither Mom nor Dad liked the part where you have to drop them into the water while they're still alive.

But for some reason they didn't seem to mind that day. They murdered two apiece so we could share the extra one—plunked them in the pot as easily as ears of corn, which made me feel a little sorry for corn. Their celebratory mood was sort of criminal too.

"Some holiday," Mom said. "I washed and bleached

twenty-two sets of sheets and pillowcases. And answered twenty-two sets of questions from those idiots in Sandpiper. They don't seem to be able to make a single decision without asking my opinion. It was easier in Boston, where all you had to do to avoid the tourists was stay indoors."

Dad nodded. "I tried to tell that Mr. Robertson I don't know beans about ocean fishing, but he didn't seem to believe me. He doesn't want to pay the money to sail on one of the fishing boats where someone could explain it to him."

"They want you to do *everything* for them," Mom said.

Dad sighed. "I think we need a vacation."

I was in agreement on that. I would even have been willing to stay here and run the place myself to get free of their complaining for a few days. But I didn't think I better say that. I could see it might be Mom's *final straw.*

After dinner we walked down the beach to watch Provincetown set off fireworks over the harbor. We could have watched from our own beachfront, but now that more of the cabins were rented out, Mom couldn't stand to run into the vacationers or spend any more time with them than absolutely necessary. She said they weren't "who I expected them to be." I don't know what she expected, but they seemed like regular tourists to me, people with noisy kids who basically wanted to sit on the beach all day and then grill hamburgers for dinner. She complained about all the sand they dragged in when they came up to the big house to ask for directions or extra towels or whatever. "They come up here barefooted and in bathing suits!" she'd say, as though that was shocking behavior for Cape Cod vacationers.

Anyway, we walked down the beach past a bunch of other resort hotels and cottage colonies. There were some big rocks lying across the beach not far away and we figured we'd sit there to watch the show, but when we got closer we saw that a noisy group blaring classic rock on their boombox had already claimed them. I was giving Mom a hand up over the rocks—Dad had trouble getting over them too, but I knew *he'd* never let me help him—when somebody shined a flashlight in my face.

"Kenyon! Is that you?"

I shaded my eyes. "Who is it?"

"Me! Razzle!"

When she turned the light on herself I could see who surrounded her—Billie, Rusty, a couple of the dogs.

"Hiya, Kenyon," Ezra said. He was perched up a little higher in the rocks, his arm around a redhead who I assumed must be Mimi.

We stopped then, and introductions were made all around. Billie stood up and wiped her hands on her jeans before shaking my parents' hands. "I heard you folks were fixin' up the Landmark. How's that comin' along?"

"Oh, just fine," Dad said heartily. "Good deal to do on those old cabins though."

"Don't fix 'em up too much, now," Billie said. "The touristas like their Cape Cod shacks just about fallin' apart."

"I imagine they prefer their toilets to flush, though," Mom said, trying, I could tell, to be civil. For some reason these days she was finding it harder than usual.

"Hey, I remember you," Rusty said. She was sitting on a rock and didn't stand, but reached up and grabbed me by the hand, pulling me toward her so that I stumbled a little in the sand. "You're the kid who came by the day I arrived—the photographer, right? How come you never came back to take my picture?" It wasn't hard to tell she was pretty plastered.

"I'll come by again sometime," I promised.

"You better! I'll be waitin' for you!" She began kicking Razzle's back with her bare foot. "I'll bet Raz here'll be waitin' for you too!"

"Stop it!" Razzle shoved her foot away, but Rusty started in again.

"Rusty, you're acting like a damn fool," Billie said.

Ezra tried his best to deflect an argument by pointing out that the fireworks had started. "They usually start slow, but they last a long time," he told us. "It takes all day to set up this many. Some of them have three or four separate bursts and then end up with those little stars that trail down the whole sky."

"How'd you get to be such an expert on fireworks, anyway?" Rusty grumbled. "A little pissant like you."

Mimi gasped in the ensuing silence.

At this point Mom turned to Billie and excused us. We'd planned to go a little farther down the beach than this, she lied.

"Nice to meet ya," Billie said. "Your boy's welcome at my house anytime. Been a good friend to Razzle."

By now Razzle was sitting in the sand, ignoring all of us, drawing with a stick. Ezra had gotten up and stalked off, back up to the road, Mimi following.

Mom and Dad smiled their good-byes, and we walked on down the beach in silence, Randolph following us for a little while, Billie and Rusty's voices following us for way too long. We were almost to the Truro town line before Mom exhaled loudly and said, "That's her *mother?*"

Thank God Dad, who was probably in too much pain to take in the finer points of Razzle's family, changed the subject.

"Nice dogs," he said. "Maybe we should get a dog." A subject it would take Mom a good hour to wrestle to the ground.

"Rusty isn't usually that bad," Razzle said.

We'd made a plan to meet at the Swap Shop at the dump at three-thirty so I could take some pictures there, something I'd planned to do since I first saw the place.

"Were your parents mad?" She was folding the shirts in one of the bins.

"Not exactly mad. Kind of . . . astounded, I think. Your family is so different from the people they know. The people they used to know. I mean, your grandmother is the same age as my mother, and your mother . . ."

". . . is a drunk. I know. She's usually better around the house. Not so mean to me and Ezra. Of course she and Billie are always at it." She sighed and threw down a shirt. "This time is worse than usual. Something's wrong, but I don't know what."

"Can you ask her?" I said.

She shook her head. "She wouldn't tell me. She never tells me anything important. Only silly stories about shoplifting lipstick or hitchhiking across Arizona with one of her boyfriends. She thinks I'm still a little kid."

Which is exactly what she looked like standing in front of a shelf of toys, pouting, a big stuffed dog beside her head. I raised the Nikon and snapped. She barely moved.

"Not in the mood for photos today?" I asked.

She shrugged. "I don't care. I don't feel like posing, but you can take what you want."

I took a few more shots of her inside, lining up the shoes

and putting out some new glasses, but it was hot in the Swap Shop and there was a nice breeze blowing outside. Razzle locked up and we went out.

"Over there. Next to those crushed squares of metal."

She nodded. "I always liked those too. I think they'd make nice tables if you could enclose them in glass or something, so you wouldn't cut yourself on the sharp edges."

"They would," I agreed. "But they wouldn't look as dramatic trapped under glass." The compacted squares were all different, some full of Folger's coffee cans, others Bud Lite and Diet Coke. The bright colors blurred into each other, and round can tops tied the random pieces together into compositions.

"Could you sort of perch in front of them?" I asked her. "Don't get so close you get cut."

She sat cross-legged in the dusty sand in front of three tall layers of squares. "Don't worry," she said. "I'm tough." But tough was not the way she looked at the moment.

I started out taking pictures from far enough away that Razzle was just a small human form, all elbows and knees, in front of a strange tower of junk. Little by little, I got closer. Sometimes I focused on some of the cans and just got part of Razzle's head or arm in a shot. Then finally I got her close up, staring at a Dumpster, at a dune, at me, framed by Alpo and corn cans and Dr Pepper.

I took more pictures that day than I'd ever taken of Razzle before. There was something about how at ease she was there, at the dump, alone, after hours, not posing, just being herself. I knew before I even printed them there were some wonderful photographs here. Lydia would like these. She'd say, *I'm not surprised.*

thirteen

Frank offered to show Razzle and me the "real Provincetown," so we made a plan to go the next Saturday. Razzle claimed she already knew plenty about Provincetown, but I knew she didn't go there much—between her dump duties, cooking for Billie, and going to school up-Cape, there wasn't much time or reason.

Since Frank wasn't an early riser on his day off, he said he'd pick us up at Mockingbird about ten-thirty in the morning. It was too hot for me to sleep late, though—the sun comes right in my bedroom window. As long as I was up, I decided I ought to take advantage of living on a beach. I put on an old pair of trunks and walked out on my own private strip of sand. Normally it wasn't all that private, but I guess everybody else was packing up to leave.

It wasn't until I got in the water, *after* doing the amount of hollering that's required when the water's that freezing cold, that I remembered Harley was likely to be at work in one of the cabins. Osprey was ready for tenants now—she and Mom were probably in there cleaning plumbing dirt out of the bathroom. But since Osprey was several cabins down from mine there was a halfway decent chance I could dash back to Mockingbird without an audience.

I didn't mind so much being skinny in clothes—it could even be an advantage if you were into that layered look. But in baggy swimming trunks, I looked ridiculous. My dead-white skin was stretched over a ribcage a vulture wouldn't bother with. My arms and legs were about the same circumference at the wrists and ankles as they were at the armpits and thighs. I was not prepared to run into Harley looking like an anorexic snowman.

Not that it mattered what Harley thought, I told myself as I waded back to shore. I wasn't going to show up on her radar screen even with my clothes on. She'd only been friendly to begin with because Primo was, and then, of course, because I knew about this job. And by now she probably wasn't feeling too grateful about that.

I'd seen her once or twice on Saturday mornings, lugging sheets and towels back and forth to the laundry shed; she never looked too cheerful. I don't think she was at her best in the workplace—at least not in her current position as lowest-in-the-pecking-order Birdhouse-cleaner under Mary Pat. That could make anybody grouchy.

I kept a surreptitious eye on Osprey as I made a beeline up the sand for the safety of my own place.

"I guess you don't have to work today, huh, Tarzan?"

She'd sneaked up on me from the other side. Wouldn't you think I would have at least brought a towel with me? I linked my arms across my pathetic chest before I turned around.

"Hey, there. Harley." She had on a T-shirt, but I'd have sworn the shorts were even shorter and tighter than the other pair, probably to get even with Mom for the T-shirt rule.

She grinned, looking down at my legs, then up to the swimming trunks, the partially hidden torso, and the suddenly chattering teeth. In her arms she held . . . towels!

"Oh, thanks," I said, grabbing the top one off the pile and flinging it around my shoulders. "Just what I needed." The towel was pitifully small. I'd need the whole stack to cover this much embarrassment.

"Hey! That's for Eagle! Now I'm gonna have to go get another one, dammit. Who do you think you are, the owner's son or something?" She pouted in a way that reminded me of Buffy the Vampire Slayer: *I'm not really mad, but I look adorable with my lips pursed like this.*

"Tarzan leave jungle now. Get dressed." What a cornball. I headed for my cabin, but she walked along with me.

"I hope your mother doesn't see me having a two-second conversation with you. She's on me every minute. How do you stand her?"

I shrugged. "She's okay." I can bash mothers with the best of them, but it's hard if somebody else says something lousy about yours.

"She hates me." Harley sighed.

"I don't think she hates you."

"Yes, she does. What are you doing today?"

"I'm going into Provincetown in a little while. After I get dressed," I said, stressing again my need to clothe my half-naked body.

"With *Razzle?*"

"Yeah, her and another friend."

Harley snickered. "What do you see in her?"

What kind of a question was that? "I don't see anything in her. We just have fun together. She's a nice kid."

Harley nodded. "A nice, screwed-up kid. A real fun nut-case. That's Razzle."

"I know you don't like her . . ."

She put up her hands. "Whatever. Is that why you didn't come to my party? Because she didn't want you to?"

Here was a revelation: she knew I hadn't come to her party. Ergo, I must not be completely invisible to good-looking females! "No. I just didn't know where you lived," I said. Although it was highly unlikely I would have gone, anyway. I wouldn't have known how to act at a party with people like Harley and Primo.

Frank's truck honked out front. Great. Caught in this delightful condition by someone *else*. "That's Frank," I told Harley. "I better let him know . . ."

"I'll let him know," she said, marching between the cabins and out to the street. God only knew· *what* she'd let him know. I followed her, my towel flapping behind my shoulders like a big wing.

"Tarzan isn't dressed yet," Harley announced through the truck window. Razzle sat in the passenger seat staring at me as I approached, not at all pleased at the scene before her.

"I thought you were riding your bike down here," I said.

"Frank picked me up on the highway." Her attention was on Harley now—the two of them were trying to eyeball each other to death.

"Just give me two minutes," I said. "I'll be right out."

"Take your time. We got the whole day in front of us," Frank said.

Then, before I could race into Mockingbird, Harley called me back, loudly. "Kenyon, I'm giving another party next Saturday night. Will you come this time? I'll make *sure* to give you directions." She was standing on one leg, like a stork. The other foot had left its sandal below and was balancing on her upper thigh. At the same time she lifted the pile of towels up to rest on top of her head. Without the ter-rycloth shield you could tell—there was nothing under that T-shirt. Nothing but *her*. She knew I knew—I could barely take my eyes off her. She gave me a huge Julia Roberts grin.

"Sure. That sounds great," I said, immediately forgetting I'd be an out-of-place stranger. I must not look *that* bad without clothes.

"See you later then," she said in a singsongy way as she swished past me, the towels once again cradled against her chest. Just watching Harley walk put a twitch in those baggy swimming trunks. I hurried inside so Razzle wouldn't notice.

Razzle was in the middle of the front seat, scooted as far over toward Frank as possible. "I can't believe you!" was the first thing she said to me when I crawled in beside her.

"What?"

"*What?* You're going to a party at Harley's! I thought you had more sense!"

She could be so annoying. "Why shouldn't I go? I'll meet some other kids."

"Oh, yeah, *her* friends. That's a select group."

"What's your problem, anyway?"

Instead of answering she raised her arms behind her head and put a big, fake smile on her face. *"Do you need directions, Kenyon? Do you need directions to my boobs?"*

Frank chuckled. I tried not to blush. "Are you mad she didn't ask you? You could probably come too if you want," I said, although I hoped she wouldn't. I really liked Razzle, but she *was* a weirdo and I didn't necessarily want to be linked with her in the minds of everybody I met.

I needn't have worried. "Are you kidding? I wouldn't go if you paid me. Besides, the only reason she asked you was to make me mad."

Okay, that made *me* mad. "Oh, sure, that's it. She couldn't possibly have invited me for any other reason, could she? Just to piss you off. God, Razzle, you think the whole world revolves around you!"

"You're the one . . ."

Frank pulled the truck over onto the shoulder. "Hold it! I'm not spending the day with the two of you yanking each other's chains. I mean it. Are you gonna call a truce or do I turn around and drop you back at the Birdhouses?"

We glared at each other silently for a few seconds, but that felt so stupid I had to laugh. "Truce?" I said. "I won't mention Harley if you won't."

"Fine," she agreed, but I had the feeling she hadn't put the subject entirely out of her mind.

By the time we got to Provincetown we were okay again. It was a beautiful day, and the streets were packed with cars, bicycles, and pedestrians. We passed several parking lots with FULL signs already blocking their entrances.

"Billie won't come here between April and December," Razzle said. "Too many people."

"That only leaves three months," I said.

"She's not a fan of P-town anyway. Too many crazies, she says."

Frank made a hmmffing noise, but didn't comment. I'd met Billie too—I figured I knew what he was thinking.

"Where the hell are we gonna park?" Razzle wondered.

"Don't worry. I've got clearance to park at the best place in town," Frank said. He turned the truck down into the center of things, wove carefully through an intersection mobbed with hotdog- and ice cream–eating families, and drove onto the main town wharf that extended out into the bay.

"You can park out here?"

"Sure. My family's full of fishermen, don't you remember?" He pulled the truck up in front of a big black boat that had ropes and nets hung all over it. It wasn't the most beautiful boat I'd ever seen, but it was certainly impressive. Not the kind of craft that had a playful name like *sunfish* or *catamaran,* this was a working boat and you could smell it from the dock.

"That's our trawler, the *Juliet,*" Frank said proudly. "Come on." He walked down a narrow dock and then made an agile jump over the side of the boat and onto the deck. Razzle followed him, nearly as gracefully. I, of course, stumbled going over the side and would have cracked my knees onto the deck floorboards if Frank hadn't been standing there to break my fall.

"Real sailor you got there," came a voice from the wheelhouse. A small man with a bushy beard appeared.

"Hi, Dad. I brought you a couple of deckhands." Frank introduced us to him as Manny Cordeiro, the best fisherman in Provincetown.

"One a' the last, anyway," Manny said, putting a hand on Frank's arm. "How you doin', Frank? You haven't been around too much."

"I had dinner with you Tuesday night!"

"Once a week isn't so much. You live half a mile away, you can come visit more than once a week."

"We've been busy, Dad."

"I didn't say *we.* I'm sayin' *you.*"

Frank sighed. "I've been busy. I'm working for Kenyon's parents down in Truro."

Manny shook his head. "Truro. Bein' bought up by Yuppies."

"Yeah, well so is Provincetown, in case you haven't noticed."

"I've noticed, don't you worry." He frowned and scratched his beard.

It was kind of nice to see that Frank didn't get along so great with his dad, either. I mean, they probably loved each other or Frank wouldn't see the guy every week, but spending time together didn't look like an easy job.

We didn't stay long. Frank gave us a brief tour of the *Juliet* and made a big deal about this 30,000-pound fish icebox they've got onboard—his dad could have talked about that for hours—and then we crawled back onto the dock and waved good-bye to Manny.

"You come by the house and see your stepmother, too!" Manny ordered.

"I will," Frank told him, then turned to us and whispered, "next month."

As we walked back up the wharf the town spread out before us along the waterfront. Even with all the tourists and shops, from here it was still a beautiful place. Boats in the harbor and houses rising up the short hills from the water—it was a postcard town. Better than postcards, though, were my own pictures; I took half a roll.

"You know, that tower, the Pilgrim Monument, is a copy of one they have in Florence, Italy," Frank said, pointing to a tall, skinny monument in the center of town. "I'd like to go there sometime and see the original."

"Why do you need to go so far away to see that one if you've got your own right here?" Razzle said.

Frank laughed. "Maybe that's why I never bothered."

We had lunch at Mojo's, Frank's favorite place, just off the wharf. It's basically a takeout window with a few tables, but it gets crowded because they have the best cheap food in town, Frank said. Of course, he knew the owner so he just went in and got us our burritos and drinks without the wait. It seemed like Frank knew everybody in town. He talked to old guys in dirty gray pants and women pushing strollers and gay couples sitting on the benches in front of Town Hall. It was like walking around with a celebrity.

After lunch we set off up some of the narrow streets that wind from the downtown into the residential areas. Small clapboard houses, painted white or weathered gray, lined the lanes up there.

"That's where I grew up," Frank said, pointing to another street of simple houses. "The one with the green door. Dad and Evelyn and my youngest brother still live there."

"Wanna go visit?" I said.

Frank groaned. "Not unless you want Evelyn to force-feed you clam pie."

"How many brothers and sisters do you have?" Razzle wanted to know.

He pretended to count them up. "Eight, last time I checked."

"Eight!" I couldn't imagine.

He nodded. "Fishermen have lots of kids. That way your crew's always part of the family."

He turned up a road that led through a small hillside cemetery. A lot of the stones were old and worn, some of them even falling over backward. "Here's your picture," Frank said, stopping on a rise and pointing west.

I stood next to him, looking out over the cemetery and down through the town to the harbor and out to sea. He was right. I took the shots. "You must come up here a lot," I said, "to know where the best view is."

He nodded. "When I was a kid we used this as our park. We'd pick a name off a gravestone and pretend to be the ghost of that person. Sounds weird, I guess, but we loved it. We'd put on plays up here, just for ourselves, where the characters were all the ghosts of somebody or other." He turned around and pointed to a small, flat grave just behind us. "This guy here, he was my best friend back then. Now I come up and visit him most days."

He said it so calmly I was stunned. The name on the grave was ANGELO FLORES, but I didn't see the dates because I didn't think it was right to stare.

Neither Razzle nor I knew what to say. I don't think Frank expected us to say anything, though. He started back down into town right away, and we followed along behind him, not even talking to each other. I'd been starting to feel like I knew Frank. His homosexuality was no big deal to me anymore—I hardly even thought about it. I knew more about his plumbing business than I ever thought I'd want to. And now I'd even met his dad, the fishing boat captain.

But this seemed like a big thing I didn't know. And the more I thought about it, the more I realized there were layers to Frank, probably layers to most people, that I wouldn't get to know in a couple of weeks, or maybe even a couple of months. If you really wanted to know somebody, I thought, it could take a long time, and it might not be so simple.

We wandered through a few shops then—Frank knew which ones had the kind of cheap, funky stuff Razzle would love. She bought a pair of wax lips, some glittery pens, and a button that said, *I'm straight but not narrow.* I looked through the bookstore for a while. And then Frank said we had to make one last stop.

We followed him into a place called the Dunelight Gallery, which was displaying a photography show. Whoever had taken the photos was technically brilliant, but I wasn't too crazy about the subject matter.

Frank walked up to a man sitting behind a desk and laid a hand on his shoulder. "Kenyon, Razzle, I want you to meet my friend Peter. He owns the gallery."

"I've been hearing so much about you two," Peter said, smiling at us like we were his birthday presents. "Finally I get to lay *eyes* on you. Frank tells me you're a photographer, Kenyon."

Peter was good-looking. He wore a very soft-looking shirt I couldn't have told you the color of—a sort of pinky/browny/grayish color. Shirts like that were expensive—you just knew it. I felt a little embarrassed, first of all trying to figure out if the relationship between Frank and Peter was what it seemed to be, and second, being called a photographer by someone who actually knew what the word meant.

"Well, I do take pictures," I admitted.

"What do you think of this show?" Peter asked.

"It's pretty good. I'm not that interested in old machines and factories though."

Peter laughed. "Me either! But some people love this guy's stuff," he said, then turned and ran his hand lightly up Frank's arm. "You'll have to get Kenyon to bring some of his work in to show me sometime. I'd love to see it."

That clarified things a little bit. I looked at Raz to see if she thought what I thought, but it was never easy to figure out what was in her head. Frank spoke to Peter in low tones while we looked at the rest of the gallery, and then we left and headed back for the truck.

We hadn't gone half a block before Razzle asked Frank, "So, is Peter your lover?"

Frank *did* blush. "Well, yes, he is."

"I like him. Do you live together?"

"You come right to the point, don't you, Raz?" Frank said. "I'm glad Peter has passed your inspection, and, yes, we do live together. We have a small house in the west end of town. And that's all the questions I'm answering today." Frank shook his head and looked at me to join him in his amazement at our friend. I shook my head too.

Razzle gave Frank a big smile. "Oh, well, there's always tomorrow."

fourteen

After our day together in P-town I was eager to spend more time with Frank. We were getting down to the last few cabins by then; I hoped the plumbing in Cormorant and Finch was really lousy so we'd have a little longer to work side by side. Before Saturday I'd seen Frank as this carefree kind of guy—work all day, play all night, or something like that. But now that I'd met his father and Peter, and seen the *Juliet* and the grave of Angelo Flores, Frank had become almost mysterious. It seemed that the more I knew him, the less I knew him.

By the middle of the next week I'd set up to paint the living room of Finch while Frank wrestled with the bathtub. Apparently my wish had come true—not only was there a leak in the tub drain, but some bozo vacationer had glued sand dollar shells all over the tub floor. Everything had to be replaced, which meant ripping out the surrounding wall tiles, too—Frank had already spent the whole day before banging away in there.

Dad, who by now was bored silly with lying on special mats and reading *Smithsonian* magazine, was spending his free time indulging a suspicious streak I'd never noticed before we moved here. He'd decided that I was too friendly with

Frank. How could I be keeping a proper eye on him if I liked him enough to hang around with him on my day off? He figured Frank had duped me into letting him goof off on the job by plying me with burritos or something.

So Dad was coming down to "help" me. His back was a little better, I guess, but he still couldn't stand up for more than twenty minutes at a time without pain, so I didn't know how he expected to paint walls. And he was cutting into my time with Frank too—we'd never be able to talk with him around.

I clued Frank in on the whole thing. "Hey, Mr. Baker," he said when Dad appeared at the door, "I hear you're gonna help us out today."

"I'll see what I can do," Dad said, barely looking at him. "Doctor said I should start using my muscles a little bit."

"I don't think he meant doing a big job like this," I said.

Dad gave me a poison look. "Are you telling me what to do now?"

"No, but . . ."

"You'll ease back into it, Mr. Baker," Frank said. "Do as much as you can do."

Dad gave him a brief smile. "That's just what I intend to do."

I'd set a can of white paint on the top of a stepladder so he wouldn't have to bend over to reach it. "Why don't you just do the middle of the walls, Dad? I'll get the top and bottom."

"Won't that look kind of slapdash?" he asked.

"This paint covers pretty well," I lied. *Slapdash?* Before all he wanted was for me to get the job done. He probably thought he was imparting some indirect message to Frank about doing things the correct way.

We worked pretty well for a while. Dad even chatted to

Frank about overflow drains and P-traps, whatever they are. When he slowed down a little I knew he must be hurting, but he kept on painting so I didn't dare say anything. By that time Frank had gotten all the pipes unhooked and was ready to move the tub out. He had a dolly to get it outside to the truck, but it would take both of us to maneuver the thing onto the dolly. "Gimme a hand, Ken," he called.

No sooner was I wedged in behind the tub than Dad appeared in the doorway. "Let me give you a hand too," he said. "It's too heavy for you and a boy to manage."

I couldn't believe it. "Dad! Are you crazy?"

The look he gave me led me to believe he was, and also that I'd better not mention that possibility again.

"Mr. Baker, this thing weighs a ton," Frank told him. "Somebody with a back problem . . ."

Dad took a giant inhale. "I could help you balance it. I wouldn't bear the weight of it. Just help you . . ."

Frank shook his head. "If the weight shifted . . . I don't want you to get hurt . . ."

"But it's all right if my son gets hurt?" Suddenly he was going off the deep end, his voice careening up and down the scale.

"Dad, I don't have a bad back."

"And I hope you never do! I just hope you never have to . . ." He was backing out of the room with this wild look on his face when he hit the stepladder. White paint flew in every direction, all over the walls, all over the dropcloth on the floor, all over Dad. We could hear him swearing all the way back up to the house.

Neither of us moved for at least a minute, then Frank said, "Let's get this hunk a' junk outa here. And then you take a break and go up to the house to see how he is. I'll clean up the mess in here."

"Are you kidding? He's mad as hell—I'm staying out of his way."

Frank fixed me with a flat stare. "You're gonna go up there and let the guy scream his head off at ya. I mean it. You tell him you're sorry you left the ladder sitting right there in the doorway. . . ."

"It wasn't *my* fault. . . ."

Frank continued as if I hadn't spoken. ". . . And then you let him bawl the hell out of you. Call you every name in the book."

"*Why?*"

"Because he's in a lot of pain, Ken, and not just his back, either. He's gotta scream at somebody. And it won't kill ya."

I gave up. We lifted that sucker onto the dolly first try.

I didn't see Harley all week. And, of course, Razzle kept asking me: *What time does that party start on Saturday? Have you gotten those directions yet?* I tried to ignore her, but she's a hard person to ignore.

I was starting to think she might be right—Harley had only asked me to annoy her enemy. But then Saturday morning Harley came by Mockingbird. Fortunately, this time I was dressed.

"This is your own little place, huh?" she said. "Cool. Very cool." She looked around my kitchen. "Do you cook stuff?"

"A few things. Eggs. Pasta. I like to eat here if I can rather than go up to my parents' house."

"*That* I can understand." She opened the refrigerator to peruse my orange juice and yogurt supply.

"Not because I don't like my parents. I just like . . . being alone."

She opened her eyes wide and laughed. "You are so *strange*."

Not the impression I'd hoped to make.

"Anyway, I can't stay in here or your mom will fire my ass for sure. I just stopped by to say Primo will pick you up around eight. Be ready."

"That's nice of him," I said.

"Yeah, it's *real* nice of him," she said, laughing again. "That Primo is *so* nice. You kill me, Kenny."

She wiggled her fingers as the screen door banged behind her, and I watched her sway down the beach. I didn't know why, but I *killed her*. It was a start.

Primo honked at eight on the dot. I'd been trying on clothes for an hour, but I was ready. I'd decided to go for the nonchalant look, which was pretty close to my old invisible look: jeans, black T-shirt, weak smile. Hey, you can't change yourself overnight.

"Thanks for the ride," I said the minute I got in, like he was somebody's mother picking me up for a Cub Scout meeting.

"No problem."

"I don't know where Harley lives," I said.

"Yeah," he said. "I do."

I couldn't seem to get a conversation going. Then I noticed the guitar and amp in the backseat. "Is your band playing again tonight?"

"Yup."

"Oh, good—I was hoping I'd get to see you play."

"Yeah."

This wasn't the same easygoing guy I'd met before. He chewed his cheek and stared out the front window. "Is there something wrong?" I finally asked.

Primo sighed and shrugged. "Not really. I'm just thinking I'm a chump to actually be *driving* you to this party at which you'll be stealing my girlfriend."

"*What?*" He must be joking.

"Yeah, I know." He gave a short laugh. "You don't even know it's gonna happen. I guess that's why I said I'd drive you—it's not your fault. That's just how she is. I've been expecting it anyway—it's been almost two months."

"I really don't know what you're talking about, Primo."

He looked at me. "This whole party thing is happening because she wants you. It's just a way to get you over to her house. She'll make the rest happen. Believe me—you won't have to do a thing."

"You're crazy! She doesn't even like me!"

"You can't always tell right away with Harley. You can't tell when it starts, or sometimes even why. Same way when it ends."

"No, no, really. You're mixed up about this. Girls never like me *that* way. I'm not good-looking enough—especially for somebody like *Harley.*"

Primo looked at me. "You look okay. Besides the big appeal for Harley is that you're new. You're different. You're from Boston, the big city, the outside world. Where she wishes she was."

There was nothing to say. Primo must be delusional. I sat staring ahead.

"Lemme just give you one piece of advice, Ken. You probably won't take it, but I'm gonna give it to you anyway. *Don't fall for her.* Date her, have sex with her, whatever. But don't fall in love with her."

Have *what* with her? Primo obviously didn't understand he was talking to someone who was a virgin at *kissing*. By the time we parked in front of Harley's big square house I could hardly hear for the odd ringing in my ears, like a high-pitched voice saying over and over, *You won't have to do a thing!* I hoped the voice was right, because I was hardly *able* to do a thing, including climb out of the car.

Primo didn't even look for Harley, just started setting up his stuff on a patio in the backyard. A couple of his bandmates had already arrived, and he didn't introduce them to me. There was a table full of junk food set up in the walk-in basement and a couple standing in front of it munching chips. Since they were the only other people I saw, I figured I might as well try to talk to them.

"Hi," I said. "My name's Kenyon. Ken."

"Hi," the girl said simply, offering no name for herself. She was busy chewing.

The guy had a cigarette in one hand and a beer in the other. "Dan," he said finally, after a good long look at me. "Who are you?"

I assumed he didn't want me to repeat my name. "I'm a friend of Harley's," I said.

"Yeah, I figured that," Dan said. "We're all friends of Harley's."

"I just moved here in June," I said, trying to give myself a reason to exist. "Razzle Penney introduced me to Harley and Primo. . . ." Her name slipped out before I remembered about keeping those origins quiet.

The chewing girl woke right up. "*Razzle Penney!* God, I haven't even thought of her in *years!* Does she still live around here?"

Dan answered for me. "Yeah, I saw her at the dump about a month ago. She works there."

"She works at the *dump?* That figures. She is so completely weird!"

"Remember that time in grade school when she put the class rabbit outside and told it to run away? And everybody was crying?"

"And when she wore those rubber waders to the first seventh-grade dance?"

"Oh, remember that time she . . ."

They wandered off then, deep in their memories of how Razzle's oddness had enhanced their youth. I would have liked to hear a few more stories of Razzle's outrageousness, but not told by their scornful voices.

People began to drift in, but nobody seemed too excited to be there. It seemed as if this was a place they came often when there was nothing else to do. They were glad to have it, but it wasn't quite enough to stave off their boredom.

Primo's group began to play, and they were pretty good. People danced, also without much energy. Where, I wondered, was Harley? I didn't know anybody else there, and after my experience with Dan and his girlfriend I didn't feel like making much effort. By nine o'clock I was beginning to think some joke was being played on me. Here I was, alone as usual, standing by myself in the middle of a party, feeling stupid. I'd even gotten my hopes up a little bit after all that crap Primo told me. I would have left immediately if I'd had a clue how to get home. Instead I walked around to the front of the house and sat on the front steps—better to feel stupid without an audience.

"There you are!" Harley came swinging up from the backyard wearing a red halter dress that could not have been shorter or tighter. "Primo said you were here, but I couldn't find you."

"I've been here an hour already and I don't know a soul. Where were you?"

"Getting ready. You want me to look my best, dontcha?" She bit her lip and smiled.

There was certainly no bra underneath that dress, and only a little red ribbon tied behind her neck to hold it up. Stop staring at her, I told myself, but it was impossible—my eyes were no longer linked to my brain. Nothing was linked to my brain. I really don't know how it happened, but somehow I was on my feet, and Harley was moving in, closer and closer to me, until she had her arms around my waist and those barely hidden breasts were tickling my stomach.

"You know, I gave this party just for you," she said. "So we could dance together. Want to?"

My tongue was not forming actual words by this point, but I did manage to put my arms around her back and shuffle my big feet a little.

She moved us away from the front door, into the shade of a willow tree. "I like this, dancing by ourselves. Don't you?"

Like it? I was awash in joy! Only in my dreams had I imagined anything like this—a beautiful girl throwing herself into my arms wearing little more than a scarf over her entire body! I was also fairly terrified.

By the time she started to kiss me, I was shaking. What a stupid wuss. She must have known I didn't know what the hell I was doing. It didn't take too long, though, to figure out the basic strategy involved. Nose to the side, mouth open—go for it.

She laughed sweetly and kissed me some more. I was actually starting to panic standing there with her wrapped around me—my arousal meter had gone from zero to sixty in just under a minute, and something had to, pardon the pun, *give*. Somehow I managed to convey the message to Harley that I needed to use the facilities, and we stumbled back into the party so she could point me toward the bathroom. *Point* being the operative word.

The rest of the evening passed in a fabulous blur. I danced, I drank, I kissed, and I did all of this with a gorgeous girl. I was a new me. A visible me. Harley introduced me to some of her friends, and I pretended I did this all the time. The new me: Party Guy.

"You're such a cutie," Harley whispered as we passed in front of the band.

I grinned nervously, glancing up at Primo.

"You *are*," she said, licking my ear. "If I say it, it's true."

Wow. I wanted to believe her, but I kept catching Primo's eyes, which were repeating what he'd told me earlier: *Don't fall for her.* Advice he obviously wasn't able to take himself. I felt bad that he'd been hurt by Harley, but he'd seen it coming—he told me that weeks ago. They were over. And, amazingly enough, it seemed to be my turn.

With her brand-new driver's license, Harley chauffeured me home herself after the party. I tried to say something to Primo before we left, but he made himself busy putting equipment away.

"Don't worry about Primo," she told me. "He's a big boy."

"I know."

"Besides, he's had two turns already. More than most guys get. He knows how I am. It's so boring living out here, seeing the same people year after year. I need somebody new, and you, Kenny, are very new."

"Thank God for that," I said.

She laughed at me again—I was starting to like it. "You are adorably strange," she said. "And weirdly different. And just what I need."

fifteen

When I called Billie's house on Sunday evening, Rusty answered.

"Hi, Sweetie," she said, after I'd asked for Razzle. "You must be that boy photographer. Since there haven't been any *other* boys around here lately. Probably not since I was a teenager." Her laugh was slightly hysterical.

I could hear Ezra in the background. "Who is it? Is it Kenyon? Gimme the phone."

"Kenyon!" Rusty said. "That's your name!" There seemed to be a struggle going on for the receiver.

Ezra came on. "Ken? She's out in the playhouse. Hold on while I get her."

Of course Rusty picked up the phone again as soon as he left. "A girl her age sitting around in a kid's playhouse—have you ever heard of anything like that?" I didn't answer her since it was obviously a trick question. She tried again. "So, do you like my little girl, Ken?"

"Sure," I said. "She's a good friend." I was hoping to head off any more embarrassing questions she might be coming up with, but, like her daughter, Rusty wasn't easily side-tracked when she had something on her mind.

"*How* good a friend, Ken? Do ya curl up in that little playhouse with her?"

A strangling noise was still caught in my throat when Razzle pulled the phone away from her mother.

"Go away, Rusty!" I could hear Raz yelling. "And stop drinking! And *leave me alone!*"

There was a long silence then before Razzle came on the line. "Hello? Kenyon?"

"She's pretty out of it tonight, huh?" I said, hoping Razzle hadn't heard her mother's final comment and therefore wasn't as humiliated as I was.

"She's such a mess! I don't know what to do. Billie doesn't even come home from work until late now, and Ezra's threatening to move in with Mimi if Rusty doesn't leave. Ez was right this time—I wish she hadn't come."

"No wonder you're hiding out in the playhouse."

"I'm not exactly hiding. I'm working on something. It's kind of a secret."

"Oh . . . okay. Anyway, the reason I called . . ." This was going to be hard, especially since things were so rotten at Billie's these days. Even without all that, she'd be mad at me. But what could I do? I really liked Harley now, especially after spending the whole day at her house lounging around pretending to watch movies, which is a great cover for making out.

What happened was, Harley asked me about my photography—maybe I was bragging about it a little bit. Anyway, she asked me what kinds of things I took pictures of, and I mentioned that I'd been taking pictures of Razzle.

"Razzle! Why her?" The Buffy-pout returned. "Wouldn't you rather take pictures of me? I'm much more photogenic. People are always telling me I could be a model!"

She *was* prettier than Razzle, but, while that was great in a girlfriend, it wasn't so important to me in a model. Razzle's strangeness really photographed well, and so did her . . . I don't know how to explain it . . . maybe it's what some people call *soul*. Anyway, she told a good story on film.

But if you suddenly have a beautiful girlfriend who wants you to take her picture, are you going to say *no?* I don't think so. Harley and I had made a plan for Monday afternoon, and, I hoped, many afternoons after that. I could still take photos of Razzle once in a while—I intended to—I just couldn't spend so much time with her anymore. But I knew what Raz would think—that I was trading her in for her archenemy. There wasn't really a *good* way to tell her.

"The reason I called was . . . umm . . . we didn't have a plan to take pictures tomorrow afternoon, did we?"

"Not a *plan*. Did you want to do something else? We could ride over to Race Point and look for weird stuff on the beach. After that rain this morning we might find . . ."

"No. I can't. I mean, the thing is, I made another plan. With . . . somebody else."

She was quiet for so long I wondered if she was still there. "Razzle?"

"Who?" she said quietly.

"Who?" I echoed. This was the hard part. "Just somebody . . ."

"It's Harley, isn't it?"

"Why do you . . . ? Okay . . . yeah. It's Harley." Why did I feel like I was betraying her? It's not like she was my girl-friend.

"I knew it," Razzle said. "That scumbag, trashball slut!"

"Razzle, stop it—it's not like that. We're just taking some pictures."

"You're taking *pictures* of her?" The phone banged down

hard enough to give me permanent ear damage. At that, I figured I was lucky.

Since I suspected Mom would be even less pleased to see me getting into a car with Harley than she was to see me riding bicycles with Raz, I told Harley to just stop quietly in front of Mockingbird, no honking or anything, and I'd watch for her. By late afternoon Mom was usually lying down with what she called a "sun headache" anyway. This idyllic retirement seemed to be killing both of my parents.

Harley was driving her mother's new VW bug, and there was a red rose in the little car vase. I was hoping she'd wear the red dress again, but I guess that was for special occasions. Today, as usual, she had on very short shorts and a tank top, without a hint of any other garment underneath. I wasn't sure I'd ever get used to that. It made me feel like my eyes were darting all over the place, trying to look and not look simultaneously.

She wanted to go to Longnook Beach, a place I'd seen only from its parking lot. "This is my favorite beach," Harley said. "It's so steep you can practically roll down the dune."

The drop from the parking lot to the beach was, indeed, very steep. Going down would be fun, but getting back up, especially with a couple of beach chairs and a cooler, must be a challenge for elderly tourists.

"Wait," I said. "Let me go ahead of you and take a few pictures as you walk down the dune."

"Sure!" Harley was so delighted with the idea that I was taking photographs of her—you'd think I was Richard Avedon or something. I ran about a quarter of the way down the dune and turned around. Harley was standing motionless a few feet from the top, one hip thrust out to the side, head thrown back dramatically. Posing.

"You don't have to pose. Just walk down naturally. Or you can stop and look at something, but just walk like you normally would."

She didn't really understand the directions. Her image of what we were doing seemed to call for a guy holding a big fan off to the side that would blow her hair all around. Lacking him, she tossed her head wildly.

"Natural," I kept saying as I backed down the dune, but natural didn't seem to be a concept Harley understood. So what? Here I was on an ocean beach on a summer day with a beautiful, braless girl who seemed to actually be my girlfriend. Had a stranger thing ever happened? Not to me.

There were a couple of eight-year-old girls making a fort near the bottom of the dune who were enthralled by the scene: Harley, heavily made up and barefoot, vamping her way down the sand hill—me, capturing every twist and pout on film. I don't know if they thought they were watching a *Vogue* fashion shoot or just a couple of deranged vacationers.

"Will you take our pictures too?" one of them asked. Immediately they both stood on their tiptoes and began to sashay around their fort in imitation of Harley's walk. It was priceless. I took a dozen pictures of them and would have taken more, but Harley was getting a little annoyed.

"I thought you came here to take pictures of *me*," she said.

"Right," I agreed. "Pictures of you." The kids traipsed after us for a while, but when we ignored them they ran back to their building.

"How about if I just sit down for a while?" Harley said, as she arranged herself prettily in the sand, her toes pointed just enough to flex the calf muscles in those tan legs. Normally I hated this kind of artificiality in pictures—she looked like a calendar photo. People didn't look perfect, and it wasn't interesting to see them try. But Harley wanted to pose for me. How could I refuse her? I could take serious pictures another time.

"Tell me what it's like to live in the city," Harley said. "Didn't you hate to leave?"

I shrugged. "At first I didn't want to leave. But now I'm beginning to like it here pretty much." I meant it as a compliment to her, but she didn't get it.

"Just wait—you'll get sick of it in no time. It's too small and there's nothing to do. I'm *dying* to get out of here and move to Boston. Or New York—that might be even better." She tossed her hair forward so it fell like a veil over one eye. I pretended to snap a few shots, but it really looked too silly.

"Cities can be lonely," I said, as if I were an expert on city life.

"*Any* place can be lonely," she said. "Nothing is lonelier than living someplace where everybody's known you since you were *born*."

I laughed. "That doesn't make sense. If everybody knows you, why should you be lonely?"

She brushed her hair back to think about that. "I guess because they don't want me to ever change. I want to be *more* than I am here. But nobody gets it. I'm not really lonely for other people—I'm just lonely for myself."

I put the camera down and looked at her sitting there so perfectly, drawing little circles in the sand with her polished toes. "Maybe they just think you're already terrific the way you are," I said.

This time she caught the compliment, and her eyes came back from a long way away, and she smiled.

"You're so sweet, Ken." She rearranged her legs and brushed some sand off her ankles. "Hey, did you tell Razzle what you were doing today?"

Ugh. A topic I'd rather not recall. "Yeah. I called her last night."

"What did she say when you told her you were taking pictures of *me?*" Harley sat forward eagerly to hear the answer, grinning.

"Does it matter?"

"I want to know!"

"Well, she wasn't too happy about it," I said.

"But what did she *say?*"

I felt like a louse repeating our phone conversation, but I had to tell her something. "She said, 'You're taking *her* picture!' and then she slammed the phone down on me."

"Hah!" Harley seemed so pleased, I wondered again if Razzle could possibly have been right, that Harley's only interest in me was pissing her off.

I put the lens cap on the camera and sat down in the sand next to Harley. "How come you want to make Razzle mad all the time?"

She shrugged. "It's a game, I guess. We've been playing it since we were little."

"Am I part of the game?"

"You're part of *my* game," she said sweetly, then laid her head on my shoulder. For the moment it was all the explanation I wanted.

sixteen

The next few weeks I walked around in a kind of semi-conscious dream. Harley would be waiting for me at three-thirty, the minute I got done working, so we could take more photos, or sometimes just hang out. After the first few days, she gave up being surreptitious and came early to hang around in her skimpy outfits and drive my mother insane. She'd hail her from fifty yards down the beach: "Hey, Mrs. Baker! How ya doin'?" Then she'd turn to me and laugh. "Mary Pat's got a wedgie over me being here again."

One day she wore a tiny bikini under her clothes and stripped down the minute she got out of her car. She'd warned me that she thought I should take some "swimming suit shots," but somehow I hadn't imagined the *Sports Illustrated* look she had in mind. Frank was still working in Finch, which had more problems than even he had foreseen, but he was sitting at the picnic table out back when Harley showed up. He'd seen her before, of course, but not in tiny strips of spandex, and I don't think she'd really appreciated his looks until she saw him leaning back in the sun that day, his muscles on display.

"Hiya!" she called to him, then pranced over. "How's the job going?" she asked.

"Slow," he said, then took in her outfit. "Goin' swimming?"

"Maybe," she said with a laugh in her voice. "Why don't you come in with us? You get a break, don't you?"

"No thanks," Frank said. "I just want to sit in the sun a few minutes."

"Oh, come on! Kenny'll lend you a pair of his gigantic trunks."

I'd already slipped into a pair of these, and a T-shirt to hide the worst of my skinniness. Nice to know wearing large clothes just made me look as if I was too dumb to know what size to buy.

Harley put her elbows on the tabletop and leaned her head on her hands, thereby giving Frank an unobstructed view of her breasts. "Don't be an old poop. They won't fire you for taking a little dip!"

He smiled, but there was a touch of annoyance in it. "No, they won't. Despite that, I'm not going to."

Harley gave up then, and came back to me, a little embarrassed. She took my hand. "Come on, Ken, let's leave this workaholic and go have some fun." I noticed as we walked down to the water, she stole a glance back at Frank.

"Is he married or something?"

"Nope," I said. "He's gay." I was glad I wasn't the only one who couldn't tell by looking.

She made a face. "He is? Why didn't you tell me before?"

"It never occurred to me. You hardly know him."

She looked down at the sand. "Now I feel silly. He doesn't *look* gay. He's a plumber and everything!"

I shrugged. "Well, he's a *gay* plumber."

"Damn. All those muscles . . . I was thinking *jock* not *gym queen*."

I didn't know what to say. "Frank's not a queen."

She ignored me. "Anyway, I guess that explains why he wasn't interested in me."

"Did you want him to be interested?"

She turned a dark look on me. "Ken!"

"Well, did you?"

She gave me a disgusted look. "Kenny! I flirt with everybody. You should know that by now!"

I did know it, but it wasn't one of my favorite things to dwell on. "So, why do you care if he's gay or not?"

"I *don't* care. I thought he was cute, is all. But now I know he's just another P-town hottie who's not interested in girls. No big deal. It's his loss."

Was this the way your girlfriend was supposed to act? Always on the lookout for *hotties?* Flirting with everybody in sight? It bothered me, but I tried to overlook it. I told myself I should be happy a girl like Harley was interested in me at all. Besides, sometimes she made me feel really good about myself.

For instance, she loved the pictures I took of her. She wanted copies of almost every one. They were mostly pretty silly because she was always acting in them, never just letting me shoot *her.* But she thought I was a great genius every time her cleavage showed to good advantage or her waist looked particularly thin. "You should do this for a living!" she told me more than once. It was flattering, but no more so than anything else that had to do with Harley. Just having a girl like that standing *near* me was flattering. It was more than I'd ever expected.

On Saturday mornings Harley had figured out how to time my mother's comings and goings so accurately that she knew just when she could sneak into Mockingbird for a few minutes. I was too self-conscious to stay in bed while I waited for her, so I'd get up and get dressed, but as soon as she arrived we'd go into the bedroom and make out.

"You lazy bum," she'd say, her hand on my thigh, her mouth tracing a path from my ear to my lips. "I wish I could sleep late on Saturday mornings."

My heart would start racing the minute she touched me, and I'd be like one of Pavlov's salivating canines by the time she got up to leave ten minutes later. Then she'd give me one last, little forehead kiss—as if she were saying *Good boy!*—and I'd know she was turning back into a chambermaid.

It was frustrating, of course, but for a kid who hadn't even had a real kiss until a few weeks before, it was a fairy tale, and sometimes afterward, when I looked in the mirror, I was surprised to see I was still me.

Finally Frank was working on Cormorant, the last cabin. There was less to do there than in Finch—he'd be finished by the end of the week. I was surprised at how disappointed I was. I really enjoyed hanging around with Frank, even if we weren't talking about anything much. He was an easy person to be with, and he always seemed to know what I was thinking.

When he showed up Thursday morning he had an idea. "Hey, let's you, me, and Razzle go into P-town again on Saturday. Peter's gallery has a great exhibit up now. It'll be a celebration for getting all these damn bathtubs and toilets fixed. I'll even spring for lunch at a snazzy place."

I wasn't sure. "It's no celebration for me," I reminded him.

"Why? You're almost done painting too."

"With the Birdhouses, but there are three gallons of white paint left, so now Mom wants me to do the inside of the laundry shed and then one of the bathrooms in their house. Two more weeks of work and nobody to do it with."

"Yeah, I know. I'll be back to working alone too. You've been good company, Ken. Usually the only folks who hang around while I'm working are those handyman types who think they can do my job better than I can."

"Like my dad," I said.

"Nah, your dad's okay. He's feeling old right now, is all. It happened to my dad too after my mom died, but he's better now. So, whataya say—we on for Saturday?"

I smiled. "Sure, but I don't know if Razzle will want to come. She's pretty mad at me these days."

Frank nodded. "About you and Harley?"

"Yeah. They had some childhood feud or something. They hate each other. So Razzle feels betrayed that I like Harley. I'm not saying *she* has to like her."

"How do you feel about her?"

"Which one?"

"Both of them."

"Well, Razzle—you know—I like her. She's funny and weird, and we have a good time together. But Harley, I mean . . . " I shook my head just thinking about it again. "I've never known a girl like Harley before."

"So you like her a lot?" he asked.

"Of course! Who wouldn't? She's so sexy and . . . and beautiful."

Frank started arranging his tools on the floor beside the kitchen sink. "Sexy and beautiful, huh? Those are at the top of your list of requirements?"

I sighed. "I know that sounds shallow, but I've never had a girl like that like me before. I've never had *any* girl like me, so the whole thing is a complete miracle! It's not a *bad* thing that she's gorgeous, is it?"

"No. I'm just saying I wouldn't necessarily put it at the top of the list."

"It's *not* at the top. That's just the first thing I thought of."

Frank nodded. "You don't think she's just a little bit of a flirt?"

"Oh, sure, I know. That's her reputation . . . always looking for the next guy."

"And that doesn't bother you?"

Okay, time to get on with my painting. I busied myself with prying up a lid. "I don't know. A little bit, I guess."

"Listen, I know I shouldn't butt into your business, Ken, but I like you and I hate to see you get hurt."

I gave a weak imitation of laughter. "I won't! I mean, I know a girl like that isn't gonna hang around with a guy like me forever." Although I fervently wished she would.

Frank stood with his hands on his hips. "No, a girl like that isn't, but not because she's somehow *better* than you. For one thing, she's constantly talking about how she can't wait to get out of here. To me that means she thinks the world is *out there* somewhere, and she's just biding her time with us small-town folk until she can get to it."

"I know," I said. "She always wants me to tell her about Boston. She thinks living in the city would be so great."

Frank nodded his head. "I understand that. When you grow up in a place like this, a little spit of sand with one road down the middle, you feel like you're noplace. The tourists come in acting like they're *somebody* and you start to think the only

way for you to be somebody too is to escape. Maybe it'll
work for Harley, but when I escaped I found out I didn't
really want to be anybody except who I already was. I can be
him just fine right here."

He grabbed a wrench and got down on his knees to look
under the sink. "Anyway, the other thing going on here is
Razzle. She's a very unique human being, and I don't want
to see her get hurt either."

"Harley isn't hurting her. They've just got this feud."

"I don't mean *Harley*. Jesus, Ken, are you blind?"

Maybe I was, because the next thing Frank said really surprised me. "Razzle is crazy about you. Don't you know
that?"

I didn't say anything for a minute while I tried to think if
it could be true. No. "You're imagining things, Frank. She
likes me the way I like her—just friends."

Frank shook his head. "I don't think so, Hotshot. You better
look a little closer next time you see her."

"Really?"

"That's my opinion. Why don't you call her and see if
she wants to help us celebrate on Saturday? Be good for
all of us."

If I'd really believed Frank, I probably wouldn't have had the
nerve to get in touch with Razzle. For one thing, I wasn't
sure I particularly wanted her to be crazy about me—her
normal amount of craziness was enough for me to deal with.
And besides, I had Harley now. Well, I didn't exactly *have* her,
but I was, for the moment, with her. I decided that, being gay
and all, Frank just wasn't reading the signals right. It was
probably different with homosexuals, more subtle or some-

thing, so he was seeing things that weren't there.

Instead of calling Raz and risking another chat with Rusty, I rode over to the dump on my lunch break. She was just helping Eddie Bacheldor carry a bunch of old, wrecked golf clubs out to his truck. Seeing him reminded me of Mrs. Thackery—Lydia—who'd be back in a few weeks for the Dump Dance and Art Show. I wondered if Eddie was looking forward to seeing her as much as I was.

Razzle saw me standing there, but as soon as the truck drove off, she paddled her flip-flops back inside the Swap Shop without a word. All of a sudden I felt really angry and stormed inside after her. She'd gone to hide back in the book aisle.

"What is going on with you?" I said. She was sitting on a milk crate, pretending to arrange books, and didn't look up at me. I refused to be ignored.

"Razzle, this is ridiculous. It's really pissing me off. Just because I hang around with Harley sometimes doesn't mean I don't want to hang out with you, too. Why can't we still be friends?"

She looked up at me; her eyes, which I would have said weren't any particular color at all, seemed in the dim sunlight yellow and burning. "If you're friends with Harley, you can't be friends with me."

"Why? Just because you had some fight when you were kids?"

"Forget it. I'm not talking about her."

"Is this just because she dumped Ezra?"

"If you want me to talk to you, you'll have to stop talking about *her!*" She had a large book in her hand, an old encyclopedia maybe, and she looked like she was about to heave it at me. Her hair had been newly cut and was standing straight up like the ruff of a furious dog; her cheeks were blood-red with anger. In the corners of her eyes, I could see small pools forming, which I knew she would never let fall— still, the fact that tears, on their own, could escape even that far meant that, whatever had happened between the two of them, it was clearly no joke. At least not to Razzle.

I stooped down so we were on the same level. "Okay. I won't say her name around you again. I promise."

She looked away from me, busily trying to decide where to stick the reference book.

I touched her knee and she flinched; I took my hand away. "So can we be friends again?"

She shrugged, still silent.

I pulled out my last card. "Frank would like us, you and me, to go with him into Provincetown again on Saturday. To celebrate his finishing the job at our place."

"Yeah?" she said quietly, still not looking at me.

"Yeah. There's an exhibit at Peter's gallery, and Frank says he'll take us to lunch someplace nice."

Razzle stood up then and walked back out to the drop-off table, where there were several bags of clothes waiting to be distributed. She hauled one bag inside and opened it, started grabbing out baby clothes.

"Well? What do you think?" I pressed her.

She took a deep breath before speaking, then said, "Did you know Donald Duck comics were banned in Finland because he doesn't wear any pants?"

Well, at least she was speaking to me again.

"So, you'll go?"

"Maybe."

I decided I should leave while I was ahead, or before she

drove me completely nuts. "Okay," I said. "I'll tell Frank."
Then, as I was heading out the door, I noticed two more golf
clubs lying on the drop-off table.

"You forgot to give these to Eddie," I said.

Razzle ran over and grabbed them from my hands. "These
are mine," she said. "You interrupted me, and I forgot to put
them in my office."

"What do you want them for?"

She smiled, hugging the clubs to her chest, happy to be
confusing me once again. "You'll know when you see."

"While I'm slaving away for your mother, you're going to
lunch with *Razzle?*" Harley's reaction to my news was not
good.

"She's still my friend," I said. "Besides, Frank invited us—
it's not like we planned it ourselves."

She brooded. "Frank doesn't like me, does he?"

"What? No! He likes you," I told her.

She shook her head. "Gay guys like types like *her,* mousy
and pathetic. I never figured that out. I mean, Barbra
Streisand? Gimme a break."

"That's not true."

"What's not true? Gay guys like Barbra, or Razzle's
pathetic?"

"Razzle isn't mousy or pathetic. She isn't."

Harley crossed her arms over her fabulous chest. "Oh, stick
up for her, why don't you?"

I hated having to argue with her, but it bothered me the
way she talked about Raz. "It's just because of this feud the
two of you have . . ."

Harley boiled over. "She's the one who carries it on! I

don't give a damn about her anymore! She acts like it was just yesterday we were friends or something. It was in the second grade, for God's sake! Get over it!"

Here was a news flash. "You were friends once?"

"A few years, when we were *babies*. She's blown the whole thing out of proportion."

This wasn't getting us anywhere. "Harley, I have to go. I told Frank I would."

"Go! See if I care!" She gathered her brown hair in one hand and brushed it high in the air so lovely little wisps hung down on her neck. It made me want to kiss her right there in front of Mockingbird, even if my mother did have a telescope, as we suspected, trained on us at all times.

"Don't be mad at me. We'll get together later," I promised.

She turned and wagged her homemade ponytail in my face. "Blow on my neck," she whispered, "and I'll forgive you."

Some punishment. Try and stop me.

seventeen

Razzle and I were quiet on the ride into P-town. Frank did most of the talking, pointing out the pier where he hung with his friends when he was a kid, which resorts he'd plumbed over the years, what famous painters used to live in which houses—all kinds of useless information just to fill up our silence.

"I'll park at my house today," he said. "It's not quite as centrally located, but there are times you don't feel like runnin' into your dad, if you know what I mean."

"Yeah, for me that's most of the time these days," I said, with a sour laugh.

After a quiet moment, Raz said, "I might not mind running into my dad sometime."

Frank's hands tightened on the steering wheel, his face got pale, and he didn't say anything else until we turned into his driveway. Then he put on a big cover-up smile. "You guys want a quick house tour or should we head for the gallery?"

The house was small and yellow with shiny black shutters on all the windows. I didn't want him to think we were nosy—like we wanted to see how gay people lived or something. "Whatever," I said, shrugging.

Of course there was never any filter on Razzle's curiosity.

"Yeah, I wanna see your house. I love seeing where people live."

"I do too," Frank said. "Why is that?"

"You get clues," she said.

"Clues to what?" I asked.

She shrugged. "Clues to whatever you're looking for."

The downstairs was three small rooms—an all-white kitchen with a guitar propped behind a round table, a living room with a curved couch and lots of art magazines lying around, and a small room that Frank called "our den." Two back-to-back desks took up most of the room, one of them with books and papers in neat piles, the other covered with high sliding stacks of all sorts of stuff—a wrench, some socks, and a soda can balanced on top of everything.

"Guess which desk is mine?" Frank said. "What can I say? I'm a slob. As a matter of fact, if I lived here by myself the whole place would probably look like this. But Peter can't deal with that level of disorganization. My desk is the only place that's allowed to look like the real me. Which, I'm sure, is all for the best."

He was so natural talking about the two of them living here together. I didn't think it would bother me since I liked Frank so much, but it sort of did. I guess because I'd never been in a place where two men lived together—like that—I was sort of embarrassed about it. I didn't *want* to feel like that, but I did. I think Frank caught on, because he said, "Okay, we don't have to go upstairs, do we? Just a bedroom."

I was halfway out the door already, but Razzle wanted to see every nook and cranny of the place. "It's so tiny," she called down from the top step. "It's almost like my playhouse!"

While we waited for her to come back down, Frank said, "You okay, Hotshot?"

"Sure. Why wouldn't I be?" I said. But I felt like a fake and a liar. I'd been feeling like that all morning anyway, like I didn't know what the truth was anymore. First standing in front of my little pretend house, blowing on Harley's neck like I'm an *adult* or something, like I know what it's all about—love, sex, all of it. And then feeling so uncomfortable with Razzle because I'm wondering what she's thinking, and whether I'm going to hurt her feelings somehow, which is awful because the great thing about being with her was that I could always just relax and be myself. And now I'm embarrassed with Frank for no reason at all, and he probably thinks I'm a real creep.

Finally Razzle was done with her inspection tour. At least it had put her in a better mood.

"Your bedroom has *dormers,*" she said ecstatically. "This is just the kind of house I want to live in someday."

Her mood seemed to pick Frank up too. "So did you get any clues?" he asked her.

"Well, I was a little rushed," she said, glancing my way. "But my first impression is that you and Peter are very compatible. Not on a cleanliness level, of course, but in more important ways. It's a house where people do things together."

Frank put his arm around her shoulders and gave her a little squeeze. "Wise child, aren't ya?" She didn't answer, but she moved in closer to him, as if to receive as much of his affection as possible.

"There you are!" Peter said as we entered the gallery. "Finally! I thought you'd be here earlier."

"It's Saturday, remember? Those of us not on a tourist's schedule like to sleep in a little," Frank said.

Peter ignored him and grabbed me gently by the arm. "Kenyon, I keep hearing that you're taking fabulous photographs this summer."

"Who told you that?" I asked.

Peter glanced around and then whispered, "Your plumber is a spy!"

I smiled. "I should have known."

"So, tell me about your pictures."

"Not much to tell—I'm working on some stuff."

"Don't be modest, dear. You've got to blow your own trumpet, you know. Now, you *are* going to show something at the Dump Dance and Art Show, aren't you?" His look was aiming for deadly serious, but came off more like painful eyebrows. I liked him, though—he seemed like a person it would be hard *not* to like.

"I have a series I thought I'd show. Of Razzle," I said. I turned to acknowledge her, and she was looking right at me, one of those deep eyeball-to-eyeball looks she saved to surprise you with on special occasions.

"Those are the ones I was telling you about, Peter. They're wonderful."

"I can't wait to see them," Peter said. "I show a lot of photography here, you know. If they're as good as your plumber says, maybe I can get you into a group show here next spring. I like to showcase emerging artists early in the season."

Emerging artists? Was that what I was? I liked the idea of emerging, like a turtle sticking its head out into the daylight or a bear coming out of its winter cave.

"I'm glad you're showing the pictures of Razzle," Peter continued. "Frank says the ones of the other girl are much more ordinary. Right, Frank?"

I froze. Please don't say anything else, I begged Peter silently. *Please.* Razzle had just started to act normal again!

Frank must have seen the look on my face, or maybe there was an equally awful expression on Razzle's face—I didn't dare look at her. Anyway, Frank covered it over pretty neatly. "Don't worry. Kenyon knows which pictures are the prizewinners."

I had to get out of that room for a minute, so I headed for the back room, where I could see there were photographs on the walls. This must be the exhibit Frank wanted me to see. I tried to enjoy it, but I could hardly tell what I was looking at—I just wanted to be alone to take some deep breaths.

The other three stayed up front, Raz looking at paintings, and Peter and Frank conversing in low tones. After fifteen minutes or so Frank stuck his head around the corner. "You getting hungry?"

"I guess so," I said.

"Peter's assistant is here to watch the shop so he can come to lunch with us. Is that okay?"

"Fine!" I said. I just hoped we could keep the conversation on neutral topics this time.

As we walked to the restaurant, Peter and Frank were behind Razzle and me, discussing some tax business or something, which meant Raz and I had to find something to say to each other. She went first, and surprised me by bringing up the forbidden topic.

"Do you really think the pictures of me are better than the ones of . . . her?"

No lying had to be done to answer that one. "Absolutely. Yours are great. Very strange and mysterious."

"And Harley's?"

I shrugged. "She just wants fashion shots. She likes to pose."

"No surprise," she said, but I could tell she was pleased.

"Really, Raz, you're a great model. At least for me." Then I remembered what Lydia Thackery had said. Maybe she was right. "I think," I told Raz, "you might be my muse."

At first I thought she'd grabbed my hand in a spontaneous gesture of joy, thrilled by my pronouncement. But, no, she was squeezing my knuckles so hard they were screaming. She stopped walking then and stepped in front of me, facing me, so I had to stop too. Her face was twisted in pain. Or maybe fear.

But she'd turned aside too late. Rusty, who was staggering toward us, a red scarf tied jauntily around her head, had seen her.

"Hey, Baby! It's my baby girl!" Rusty didn't stop walking until she was standing right on top of Razzle and me, her boozy breath huffing in our faces. "And, look, she's with her *boy*friend!"

Raz whispered, probably hoping Rusty would mimic her. "What are you doin' here? I thought you said you hated P-town."

"Times change," Rusty bellowed. "Time for me to change too. I'm sick of hiding out. Sick of the whole damn thing." She threw an arm around Razzle's waist, more for stability than tenderness. She had on a tiny, fake-leather skirt and one of those tube tops that looks like you're wearing a big rubber band across your chest. To top off the fashion statement, she'd bleached her hair a kind of peachy orange.

Peter and Frank pulled up behind us, Frank staring.

"My God," he said. "Rusty Penney."

Rusty stared up at Frank without recognition. "Do I know you?"

"Frank Cordeiro. You remember me," he said with certainty.

A tremor ran through Rusty's body while a look of panic crossed her face. She let go of Razzle and took a step back, as if she might run away. "Frank."

"Been sixteen years, Rusty. You haven't been around much," Frank said.

Peter inhaled deeply. "Oh, my God, now I get it." I wished *I* did.

"I went away," Rusty said, her head flopping backward as if her neck muscles had suddenly given out. "Nobody wanted me here. They said it was all my fault. *You* said it too, but it *wasn't* my fault. I didn't force him." She looked at Raz and me. "You believe me, don't you!"

I was pretty sure Raz had no idea what Rusty was talking about. Mostly she was just mortified by the fact that her drunken mother was talking loud and crazy in the middle of Commercial Street while hordes of people passed by on all sides.

"Sure, Rusty, I believe you," she said. "Maybe you should go home now. Did you drive in?"

But Rusty wasn't listening; she'd switched her attention back to Frank. "You don't believe me, though, do you? You always blamed me."

Frank nodded. "I did at the time, Rusty. I'm older now. I'm sure it was more complicated than I thought."

"It sure as hell *was* complicated," Rusty yelled back at him,

and then the tears burst out. "I didn't know he was an angel!"
She was crying so hard you could barely understand her. "I
didn't know!"

Frank stepped forward and put his arm awkwardly around
her shoulders, but she resisted him. "It's too late now," she
said. "Besides, *he* forgives me. He tells me all the time, 'I forgive you, Rusty.' I bet you've never even *seen* him, have you,
Frank? In all these years have you even *seen* him? I see him
all the time!" She was screaming again and pulling away
from us.

"Please calm down, Rusty," Razzle said.

"Have you seen him?" she stuck her face as close to Frank's
as she could.

"No, I haven't see him," Frank said.

"Then you know *nothing!*" She turned and began to stomp
off down the street.

"I talk to him, though, all the time," Frank said quietly, then
he loped down the street after her. "Wait, Rusty, I'll give you
a ride home."

She flung his hand off her arm. "I don't need your help
now, Frank."

"You shouldn't drive like this."

"I'll get a ride. Don't you worry, Frankie. Somebody is
always willing to give Rusty a ride." She laughed and walked
on, weaving away from us, high heels wobbling.

Razzle was still gripping my hand. I tried to send gentle
messages from my hand to hers to calm her down, but my
goodwill was no match for her anxiety. She was shaking so
much I started vibrating too.

If Peter hadn't shepherded us all into the closest restaurant,

Frank, Raz, and I might have stood out on the sidewalk like zombies for hours. "We need to sit down and have a drink, or, in your case, food," he said. But when the menus came and the rest of us managed to order something, Razzle said she wasn't hungry.

"How about some soup?" Peter pressed. "Soup is always good when you feel like shit, pardon my French."

She shook her head. "I don't think so."

"Bring her a bowl of clam chowder," Frank said to the waiter. Then to Raz: "If you don't eat it, I will."

But finding a topic of conversation was impossible since all any of us had on our minds was Rusty and whatever had just happened on the street. I kept trying to imagine what they were they talking about. *What* wasn't Rusty's fault? Obviously Frank had known Rusty better than I thought, and the two of them knew some kind of secret. Something happened that Frank blamed Rusty for, but what could it be? Was this about Razzle's father?

By the time the waiter set the bowl of milky clam chowder down in front of Razzle, her face was the same color as the soup. "I'm not . . . I better . . ." she said, then got up and ran for the ladies' room.

As soon as the door closed behind her, Frank exploded, "Goddamn it! What should I do? I don't know what to do!" He looked at Peter, then me, then back to Peter. People at surrounding tables were looking at all three of us.

"Well, that girl needs to know what happened. That's clear to me," Peter said. "It's making her sick not to know."

"I know, but I can't tell her," Frank said. "It's not my place. Besides, I think she's afraid of knowing the truth—especially after this."

I cleared my throat, trying to think of a way to ask, but Frank cut me off.

"And no, I can't tell you either. Not until Razzle knows."

"Why hasn't anyone ever told her?" Peter asked.

"I don't know." His jaw tightened. "This is what I'm going to do. Tomorrow morning, before Rusty can get herself tight again, I'm going up to Billie's to have a talk with her. I'll say she has to tell Razzle before she finds out some other way. She's old enough now, and she deserves to know the truth— eventually she'll meet somebody who knows the whole story, anyway."

"Like you," I said.

"Like me, with fewer scruples."

"Can I come too?" I scarcely dared ask.

Frank was already starting to shake his head no, but Peter interrupted him. "Maybe that's not a bad idea, Frank. Kenyon could keep Razzle distracted while you talk to Rusty."

"I can do that," I said. "We'll go out to her playhouse."

Frank chewed on the idea. "Yeah, maybe so. Okay, you can come. I'll pick you up at ten-thirty." He kept looking at the bathroom door. "You think she's all right in there?"

"I *doubt* it," Peter said.

None of us could manage to eat much. Nobody touched Razzle's chowder. Finally Frank decided to jog back to his house and get the truck so she wouldn't have to walk back across town. Raz was still in the bathroom when he returned, and we were starting to get worried.

Peter called an elderly waitress over and asked if she'd go in and tell the tall, thin girl that we had the truck parked right outside waiting for her. The woman would really have pre- ferred to give us a lecture on illegal parking, but Peter was adamant about Razzle's ill health, so she went in. A few minutes later Raz walked out alone—the waitress must have decided to stay in and have a cigarette or something. Razzle's face was blotchy and her eyes were red, but there were no actual tears to be seen.

"Are you sick?" I asked her.

"No," she said, looking straight ahead. "Just get me home."

The three of us got in the truck, said good-bye to Peter, and drove off. Raz fell asleep, or pretended to, before we got out of town.

eighteen

When we got to Billie's the next morning Razzle was washing a sinkful of dishes while Billie and Rusty sat on either side of a table spread with tarot cards. We could hear them arguing as we walked up to the house. The dogs came running out, of course, but their barking was no louder than Billie's.

"Jesus!" she roared. "That's the third time since you've been here you've gotten the Hanged Man for your cover card! You can run, but you can't hide, girl!"

Rusty jumped up from the table. "I didn't ask you to do my goddamn cards, did I? You're making 'em turn out like that. I don't believe in these stupid cards anyway."

"You believe in everything. That's your problem. One of many."

They both looked up when the blue screen door slammed. Raz must have seen us coming up the path—she glanced at us, then went back to her methodical washing.

"Morning," Frank said.

"Can I help you?" Billie said, then recognized me. "Oh, it's you. Who's your friend?"

"This is . . ."

But Rusty wanted to break the news to her mother herself. "Billie, don't you recognize the man? This is my dear old friend, Frank Cordeiro." She took a long drag on her smoked-down cigarette.

"Good to see you again, Billie," Frank said, tipping his head in her direction.

Billie went pale, just for a minute, then rallied. "What do *you* want?"

"I'd like to talk to Rusty, if I may."

Rusty laughed and walked over to us, dropping her cigarette into the dishwater on the way. It sizzled and went out.

"Damn you, Rusty," Raz mumbled, fishing it out.

"If you *may?*" Rusty repeated. "You've picked up a few manners in the last sixteen years, Frankie."

"I didn't come to argue with you, Rusty, or to play games. I really would just like to talk to you. Alone, if that's possible." Frank looked so serious that she stopped smiling.

"I'm outa here," Billie said. "Can't spend a minute in my own damn house anymore with all this *drama* going on all the time." She got to her feet and flexed one knee before heading for the door.

"I don't mean to chase you away," Frank said.

"Yeah, Billie, why don't you stay and do Frank's cards for him?" Rusty said, snickering.

Billie brushed at Frank with her hand. "Whatever you're here for, I don't want to listen to it. As far as I'm concerned, that subject is closed."

"Unless you're tryin' to get to me," Rusty said. "Then you're willing to bring it up."

Billie ignored her. "I'm goin' down to the flats and get some clams so there's somethin' for supper. Nobody else around here will give a thought to it."

She grabbed a pair of sandy boots from behind the door and went out, whispering to the dogs who crowded around her like orphans begging to be picked to go along for the ride.

I stood next to Razzle. "Want to come outside with me?" She didn't look up. "I gotta wash the rest of the dishes." "You can do it later. I'll help you later on."

She sighed and shook the water off her hands, reaching for a towel. She'd go with me if she had to.

Meanwhile Rusty was pouring coffee for herself and Frank, which made her seem almost normal, like an actual grownup.

I followed Raz out onto the porch, and we sat in rockers on the ocean side, where there was a little breeze blowing. Betsy-Wetsy jumped up in my lap immediately, and a beagle whose name I'd forgotten settled on Razzle's legs. Old Randolph lay between the chairs. It was peaceful sitting there, looking out at all that sparkling blue water, carelessly stroking the dogs. We were quiet for a while, but it wasn't one of those what-should-I-say-now kinds of quiet—it was comfortable.

Razzle broke the silence with a simple statement. "Ezra's gone," she said.

I looked at her, but her face wasn't giving anything away this time. "Gone?"

"Moved out. Last night. Rusty and me got into a big fight about her drinking—you can imagine—and Billie started in too, and Ez said he couldn't stand it anymore. So he's living with Mimi, in Provincetown." She bent over so the beagle could lick her chin.

I tried out a half-hearted laugh. "Well, the fight was probably just an excuse. I mean, he wanted to move in with Mimi anyway, didn't he?"

She shrugged. "Maybe. But how am I gonna live here all alone, without Ez?"

I didn't have an answer for that—without Ezra here she *would* be alone. The two of them looked out for each other. They were closer than siblings usually are because they had to be; Billie might bring home supper, but their family was each other.

"Once Rusty leaves," I said, "Billie won't be so mad all the time, right? You'll get along with her better."

She nodded. "Sure. As long as I never complain, or bother her with my problems, or ask her any personal questions. As long as I don't give her any trouble or remind her I'm related to Rusty." She leaned over farther so she could lay her head on the little dog's back.

"At least I've got these guys," she said with a laugh. As though in response, Randolph staggered to his feet and laid his big yellow head on her knee. "Billie rescued them and they rescue me, dontcha, Randy?"

It wasn't like Razzle to let herself get so down. I tried logic. "Ezra's out of high school. Most eighteen-year-olds leave home for college or a job. In two more years you'll graduate and go off on your own too."

She shook her head. "I don't want to go anywhere. I like it here."

I was shocked. "At Billie's? You want to live *here* forever?"

She thought about it. "No. I'd like to have a little house of my own, like Frank and Peter's house. That would be nice."

"Another playhouse," I said.

"What's wrong with that?"

"Nothing, except that a playhouse isn't a real house. It's living in your imagination. Of course, I realize only a Perwim like me would see anything wrong with that."

She raised one eyebrow in my direction. "Aren't *you* living in a playhouse this summer?"

I was so surprised she'd zinged me, I laughed. "Well, for the summer I guess I am, but I'll be moving into the big house— in more ways than one—by fall."

"So, at least for the summer, you have a little imagination?"

"How did this conversation get turned around to *me?*" I asked her, but before she could come up with another witty response, the screen door slammed again and the dogs leapt from our laps to run and bark with their cohorts.

"Ken! Where are you? Kenyon, I'm leaving!" I could tell from Frank's yelling that the discussion hadn't gone well. I ran around to the other side of the house, Razzle following at a distance.

"What happened?" I said as I caught up to Frank, already on his way to the truck.

"Nothing happened. And I'm gonna go nuts if I spend another minute in there going around in circles with her." He kicked his front tire and then leaned against the truck, running a hand through his hair.

"She won't tell her?"

He sighed. "No, she won't. She refuses to listen to reason. I don't know if she's mostly crazy or mostly scared. She's lived with this so long already . . ." He trailed off, remembering that I didn't know the whole story. Or, really, *any* of the story. "I don't know what else to do. Let's just get out of here."

Razzle was hanging back, closer to the house, holding the

beagle again, looking at us. Her buzzed hair was starting to grow out a little so that it laid down closer to her head. Is that what made her look so vulnerable? Anyway, I knew I couldn't just run off and leave her—not right now.

"I might stay for a while," I told Frank. "I can walk home later."

He looked surprised. "You sure? It's a long walk from here."

"I don't mind."

He clapped me on the back, frowning, and climbed into the truck, then roared down the path, ripping it up as much as Ezra usually did.

Razzle waited for me to walk back. "What's going on?" she asked, chewing a nail. "What did Frank want to talk to Rusty about?"

Surely she knew as much about all this as I did, didn't she? "He thinks Rusty should tell you something. About her past, or maybe about your father, I don't know. Something happened that they both know about . . . and you don't."

She turned aside. "Maybe I don't want to know—did Frank ever think of that? Maybe I don't want to hear some rotten story about who my dad is."

"How do you know it's a rotten story about your dad?"

"I just do!" She let the beagle drop to the sand. "Up until yesterday afternoon I was thinking maybe it was Frank. I know he's gay, but I thought maybe somehow, in the past . . . I don't know. I like Frank. It would have been great if he'd been my father. But he isn't. If he was, *he* could tell me—he wouldn't need Rusty to do it."

I figured she was right about that. "Still," I said, "haven't you ever wanted to know? Doesn't Ezra want to know?"

She sighed and glanced back at the house. "Let's go somewhere else to talk. Away from *her*."

"The playhouse?" It seemed like the obvious place, but Razzle looked startled.

"No! You can't go inside the playhouse. I'm working on something in there, and nobody can see it until it's finished."

"Well, where then?"

"Let's go down to the beach. It'll be empty." She headed back to the ocean side of the property.

Billie's house is, in a way, right on the beach—that is, there's nothing between it and the water except sand. However, the sand at this point is a dune that falls away as steeply as Longnook Beach, only it's twice as high, and the path down twists through scrubby pines and wild rosebushes before its final plunge.

"Going down looks like the easy part," I said, looking over the crest.

"It is, unless you get too close to the tern nesting area."

"Why? What happens then?"

"Ever seen that Hitchcock movie, *The Birds*?" she asked. "That's what happens."

"Great," I said, but Razzle was already starting down, so I took off my sandals and followed. We slid a good portion of the way, grabbing bushes to slow us down, then finally giving in to it and just whooshing straight down. I got going faster than Raz and bumped into her so we landed in a heap on the sand.

We just lay there laughing for a minute, and I was glad that the old, carefree Razzle seemed to have returned. "Let's do it again!" she shouted.

"Are you kidding? Climb all the way back up there just to slide back down?"

"Ez and I used to do it all the time when we were kids," she said, but just the mention of Ezra stole the smile from her face again.

We lay back against the bottom of the dune so our faces were in the shade and quietly caught our breath. There was no one else on the whole beach, as far as you could see. All the tourists would be clustered within a few hundred feet of a parking lot, and there wasn't one of those for miles.

This was the perfect Cape Cod summer day—I think I'd been spending the past few months expecting it and not quite finding it. Just me and the sun and the beach. Nothing else, except, of course, Razzle.

"You asked me before why Ezra doesn't want to know who our father is," Razzle said, bringing me back to reality. "I think he *does* know. I think he found out since he's been working in P-town. That's why he's so mad at Rusty. He hasn't said anything, but I can practically read Ezra's mind. He knows."

"And you haven't asked him?"

She shook her head. "It must be a bad story; otherwise he'd have told me by now."

"But you'll have to find out sooner or later," I said.

"I don't see why."

"Well, Raz," I said, "it's the story of your life, isn't it?"

"I'm the story of my life. Not Rusty and some guy I never met."

She wound a blade of beach grass around her hand. After a few minutes she said, almost begging, "Let's not talk about this anymore, Kenyon. Let's just have a good time today, can we? A really good time."

So we did. In fact, I think it was the nicest day I'd ever had with Razzle. First we took a long walk by the water, picking up sea glass and shells and stuffing them in our pockets, dancing back when a wave came in, then wading out and letting the next one soak us good. We built a castle and decorated it with kelp and sea lettuce and our beachcombing finds until it looked like a Las Vegas nightclub. We surveyed the tern nests from a distance, and I wished I'd brought my camera with its zoom lens so we could look more closely.

"You rely on that camera too much," Razzle said. "I'm glad you don't have it today."

"Really? I thought you liked me to take your picture."

"I do, sometimes. But I get tired of just being a *thing*, like that. A model or whatever. Something you can only see through that machine."

Once again I told her, "Mrs. Thackery says you're my muse."

She screwed up her face. "I don't know what that means," she said.

"I think it means, like, an inspiration."

Razzle's face glowed golden. "Really? I like that! I'll be your *inspiration!*" Then she smiled slyly. "Even if *she's* your model."

"I thought we weren't going to talk about her?" I reminded Raz.

We must have wandered a little too close to the nesting area because suddenly a white bird was screaming at us as it swooped low over our heads.

"We're leaving!" Razzle shouted at the tern while we ran, hands folded protectively over our heads. The bird was more than a little mad—she followed us until we were back at our original dune where we collapsed, again, in the shade.

"Okay," Raz said. "I'm going to tell you the real story, the real me and Harley story, so you know why I hate her."

I was curious, but it made me feel a little traitorous to listen to Razzle's side. "Harley said you used to be friends when you were little kids," I said.

"She admitted that, huh?"

I nodded.

"The thing was, I didn't have a lot of friends. Mostly, I think, because of having no parents around and living up at Billie's house—kids were sort of afraid to come to Billie's. And, as you know, I'm sort of different from other kids—I guess I always was."

"You're an original, Raz."

"Yeah, well, people don't like originals much. We make them nervous."

"So, Harley teased you about that?"

"Wait . . . I'm tellin' it." She picked up a handful of sand and let it run through the funnel of her fist back onto the beach. "Harley was my first and, for a long time, my only friend. In first and second grade we were like this." Two fingers of her right hand wrapped around each other to demonstrate.

"No kidding?"

"We were both wilder than the other girls—we were a great team. Harley had other friends, too—she was an outgoing kid, and pretty, too, even then."

Not hard to believe.

"So, because Harley liked me, other kids started being more friendly too. For a while there I actually had a whole bunch of friends. Or at least I thought I did." Quietly, she said, "I really sort of loved her—you know—the way kids do." She dug a hole in the sand with two fingers, like a giant bug.

"And then she dumped you?"

"Can I tell it, please?"

"These things happen with kids, Raz. They move from one friendship to another. You just took it too personally . . ."

"Were you there, Kenyon? Do you want to hear what happened or not?"

I shut up and let her finish.

"In the third grade, all of a sudden, Harley decided she was too good for me—I guess she'd noticed she was pretty or something—and she decided to find a better-looking best friend. Okay, I *know* kids do this. But Harley didn't just dump me, she also decided that nobody else should be my friend either. She made up lies about me and about Billie and Rusty." She paused for a minute, remembering the lies, and her face got tight and angry. "She said I hit her and stole things from her house, and that Billie hated me and made me sleep outside, and that my mother wasn't in Arizona—she was in a mental institution. She made us sound like lunatics. And it worked—kids were afraid of me. They wouldn't play with me if I paid them. She turned *everybody* against me."

"Okay," I admitted, "that was not nice."

"She told people I was crazy and I *got* crazy. I turned into who she said I was."

I nodded. "Look, I know you think I'm standing up for her, but I'm not. I just think if you could realize she was just a little kid too, you could forgive her . . ."

"Don't you get it? She's the really crazy one. She *still* is. Whether I forgive her or not, she's still a person who could do the very same thing today. And *does.* To everybody."

This sounded a little similar to the tune Primo had been singing about Harley, but I still wasn't interested in listening. Fortunately the weather was in on my conspiracy to change the subject. Dark clouds had covered up the sun, and it was getting chilly.

Razzle sighed, giving up on me, I guess. "These are rain clouds. We've got about a minute and a half to get up the hill before we get drenched."

Going uphill was ridiculous. For every sandy step you took forward, you slid back almost as far. Raz was more goat-footed than I and stretched a hand back to help me, but I knew I'd just pull her backward too so I struggled alone. Once we reached the bushes it was easier to hold on and pull ourselves up, but the rain had started by then. By the time we reached the top and ran for the porch, we were scratched up and soaked through.

"Jesus!" I said. "And I have to walk home in these soggy clothes!"

"The rain'll pass," Raz said, certain of it. "Then you can lie in the sun and dry out."

We were both breathing heavily from our quick climb, and I was leaning against one of the porch supports.

Between deep breaths Razzle said, "The human heart pumps so hard it can squirt blood thirty feet."

"What?"

"Wait here," she said, and went inside to get us towels.

"What's Rusty doing?" I asked as I dried my hair.

"Sleeping on the couch, as usual, with the TV blaring. Look, the rain's already heading out to sea. A few more minutes and we can lie in the sand and dry off." Sure enough, the gray patch was moving offshore, like a giant's shadow.

We put our towels down in the sand just outside the porch and sprawled, exhausted, on our stomachs. "I have to ask you something," I said to Razzle.

"What now?" Her head was turned away from me.

"Where do you come up with all this stuff about Marilyn Monroe's toes and pigs' orgasms and squirting hearts? I've never known anybody who knew so much disgusting trivia and used it so regularly."

She turned toward me, grinning. "Oh, *that*. Like it? I read this book once, a couple of years ago, that had all these strange facts in it, and I memorized it."

"The whole book?"

"Most of it. That way, I'd always have something to say in any uncomfortable situation, you know, when I wasn't sure what I *should* say. Like if I'm feeling shy or embarrassed or weird or something."

"It adds to your reputation."

She smiled. "Yeah, there's that, too."

Lying in the hot sun was making me feel so drowsy. But I still wanted to talk, like when you have a friend spending the night and it's late, but you hate to fall asleep because you know that's the end of the sleepover. I mumbled, "You could just *say* you feel shy or embarrassed or weird, couldn't you?"

Her eyes were closing, but she made a face. "I don't think so."

I made one last effort. "You could tell *me,* couldn't you? If that happened? Instead of saying something weird?"

"You want me to?" Her eyelids slipped all the way down.

"Yeah."

"Okay. I will."

We slept for hours.

nineteen

Now that Frank wasn't around, the work seemed almost unbearable. The laundry shed had only two small windows, which weren't enough to vent either the heat from the dryers or the stink of the paint, so I whitened and brightened that place in as little time as humanly possible.

By the time I got up to the big house I was sick to death of painting. The idea of spending one more day putting masking tape on window panes, then cracking open another giant can of colorless goo and slapping it around was enough to make me want to jump right *through* those window panes. The first morning I was in the upstairs bathroom, I just shut the door and sat on the toilet lid reading a *Photography* magazine. I didn't do a damn thing for hours. After that it got to be sort of a habit—most days I did more reading than painting. And the funny thing was, nobody seemed to notice. Or if they did, they didn't care.

When I'd worked on the cabins way down the beach Mom had stopped by at lunchtime every day—and Dad usually came by too unless he'd managed to come up with some job he could do himself. Even though they always had an errand that brought them there, it was clear they were checking up. On Frank, but also on me.

But now that I was in their own home, they ignored me. Not so much as an apple or a glass of tea appeared on the job site. Mom came through the kitchen one day when I was fixing myself a sandwich and said, "Oh, is it noon already? Is there anything to eat?" as though the whole idea of finding food to eat in the middle of the day was a little too exhausting for her.

I didn't mind. Better not to have them looking over my shoulder. Dad had been feeling better for a week or so, and he'd done a beach cleaning one afternoon, picking up a bunch of dead goosefish and a sticky pile of seaweed that had tumbled onshore when a high tide combined with a windy storm. Of course he overdid it a bit, and by the next day he was in pain again.

"Go lie on your mat," Mom commanded.

"Sounds like you're talking to a dog," Dad said. "I'm not a dog, you know."

I heard the beginning of this discussion while I was making my lunch downstairs. I didn't mean to eavesdrop, but I'd gotten into the habit of taking my sandwich upstairs and eating it in the room that would be mine in another few weeks when we shut up the cabins. I was trying to get used to it, get the feel of it. And if I felt like taking a short nap after lunch, well, the bed was right there, and nobody seemed to care how long it took me to finish painting the bathroom anyway.

So that's where I was when Mom finally herded Dad upstairs to their room. I guess they thought I'd gone outside or something, or maybe they'd just stopped thinking about me at all. Anyway, they left the door to their room open, and I couldn't help hearing their conversation. Dad had just groaned his way down to the floor mat and was obviously in an extremely crappy mood.

"Do you think it makes me happy to see you lying on that thing day after day?" Mom said. "It's not *my* fault you hurt yourself. This wasn't my idea of retirement either, you know."

"Excuse me for trying to lift that two-hundred-pound heirloom mirror your mother left us." Dad sounded like he was grinding his teeth together.

"Why did we have movers if you were carrying the heavy things?"

"And what would you be saying if they dropped the damn thing?"

"There's no need to swear at me, Ted!" Then she sighed. "Let's stop snapping at each other. I really can't take it anymore. I think . . ." she began, then stopped.

"You think what?" Dad said, sounding like he really didn't care. I sat forward on the bed, eager to hear what she thought, since I was not normally exposed to many of my mother's thoughts.

"I think this is not working out the way we'd hoped it would. And maybe we should just give it up. Admit it isn't working." Her voice sounded thick and snotty as if she was getting ready to cry, at which point I felt like a sneak for sitting there listening.

Nobody said anything for a minute, then Dad spoke. "Now, Mary Pat, it's not that bad."

"Oh, Ted, it's awful! The tourists are irritating, the work is endless, and we haven't even made any friends here." Now she *was* crying. "Not to mention that you're in constant pain! I don't think I can keep going much longer like this."

It was terrible to listen to my mother cry. She never did it in front of me, though I'd heard her once or twice before in my life, when someone she knew died, but even then she closed herself in the bathroom so no one else could hear much. She usually recovered pretty fast, though, so I didn't think she was really serious about giving up on Baker's Birdhouses.

Dad tried to console her, but I guess when you're lying flat on your back on the floor it's hard to sound too confident. I felt guilty for hearing all this, so I starting making some clunking noises as if I'd just come upstairs. Mary Pat shut their door then, and I didn't hear anything else.

Harley continued to show up at Mockingbird for ten quick minutes of smooching every Saturday morning. But now that I knew Mom wasn't being too vigilant about who was doing what, it crossed my mind that Harley could stay a little longer if she wanted to. I could pull down the shade and lock the door, and nobody would know *where* she was. Just the idea, however, made me so nervous I broke into a sweat and had to take a second shower before she showed up.

"Hiya," she said, slipping in the door and right into my arms. "Been waitin'?"

"Yeah," I said, unable to resist going back immediately to where we'd left off several nights before, that is, with my hands underneath her T-shirt on her unleashed breasts. It probably would have taken me another year to get up the nerve to do this by myself, but sitting in her car that night she'd taken my hands and put them there. Just like that. My God.

Of course, we could have gone inside my cabin then and had more privacy, but Harley always had an excuse why she couldn't come in at night. I never pushed her. If sticking my hands under her shirt was a consolation prize, I could live with it.

So Saturday morning I explained to her that Mom and Dad were letting up on the spy routine and that she could probably stay there with me for a half hour if she wanted to. A half hour in which we could do . . . anything.

She leaned back and smiled. "Actually, I wanted to talk to you a little bit this morning."

Talk? My hands slipped back down to her waist.

"I ran into Primo yesterday, and I guess he'd run into Razzle. And he told me that she told him that you were going to show a whole bunch of pictures of *her* at the Dump Dance and Art Show." She smiled at me adorably. "You wouldn't do that to me, would you, Ken?"

Oh, no. "Well, the thing is . . ."

"I thought *I* was your girlfriend?" The smile closed down into a hard line.

"That doesn't have anything to do with it. I have a *series* of photos I took of Razzle. They all go together." I could tell by the look on her face there was no way on earth she was going to be understanding about this.

"I believe you took a *series* of pictures of me, too, didn't you?" she asked.

I opened my mouth, but no sound came out. How could I explain the difference between the two sets of pictures? Anything I said would sound insulting.

Harley had walked away from me by now. "Do you think Razzle's prettier than me?" she asked.

"What? No! Of course not! You're beautiful!"

She stood across the room from me, her face tense, her

body still loose and welcoming. "Then why aren't you using my pictures? What has she got that I don't?"

"Nothing. Her face is interesting, that's all. She has an interesting look."

"*Interesting?* And I'm not interesting, is that it?" She folded her arms across her lovely chest.

How could I get out of this? "Come on, Harley, you know I think you're totally amazing. Let's go into the bedroom and sit down . . ."

"No thanks. Ask Razzle." She walked toward the door.

"Harley!" I was desperate; I *couldn't* lose Harley! I was crazy about her. "Look, how about if I use a few photos of you too? The best ones." I started to regret the offer immediately, but what else could I do?

"Just a few? And still use all of hers?"

I couldn't cut down the *Angel of Mysteries* series—it was perfect as it was—ten shots of Raz in the white dress, from the faraway one with all the cabins stretching out behind her, to the close-up of her eyes under a big hat brim. I couldn't imagine taking any of those shots out. But each artist only got a certain amount of space, and ten photographs used up my allotment.

"Hers *go* together," I tried again to explain.

"Half mine, half hers. That's fair," Harley said. "I just want half."

There had to be some way to make her understand. "I love the pictures of you, Harley. I do. Unfortunately, I won't have enough space for all . . ."

"Am I being unreasonable, Ken? I don't think I am. I *thought* I was somebody special to you . . ." Her eyes had frozen into ice cubes. I couldn't let this happen.

"Maybe I could make room for a few . . ."

"Half."

"Harley, this show is important to me! Frank says people come from all over to see it."

"Well, it's important to me too, isn't it? Maybe somebody will see *me!*"

I looked at her standing in the doorway of my bedroom, one hand high up on the doorframe, leaning into it. I'd just been touching her body under that T-shirt, and I was afraid I might never be allowed to touch it again. It made me break out into a sweat to remember what her belly felt like as my hands crept up to her breasts. Was the Dump Show more important than *this?*

"Okay," I said finally. "Okay. Half hers, half yours." It made me nuts to think of ripping the series apart like that, but at the moment it didn't seem like I had a choice.

The tension melted off her face. She came toward me again, encircled my neck with her arms, and gave me a kiss. "Oh, Ken, I'm so happy! I'm gonna tell everybody to come and see my pictures!"

We'd wasted half our precious time on this argument and I was eager to retire to the bedroom, but Harley held back. "You know, I have a lot of work to do this morning, but let's make a plan, huh? After the Dump Dance I'll come back here with you. We'll celebrate. We'll *really* celebrate."

She gave me a kiss that unglued my knee joints. When she disappeared out the door, I lay down on my bed. I'd either been seduced by a champion or run over by a truck—either way my body needed some time to recover.

Sunday afternoon the rain came down in sheets, and there

was a chilly wind that reminded me the end of the summer wasn't far off. Most of our guests had gone into P-town for the day to jostle for restaurant seats, or to buy a sweatshirt to replace the one they'd forgotten to pack, or to buy a book to read on the beach as soon as the sun returned. That's what you do here on rainy days.

Mom and Dad had driven off in the opposite direction, up-Cape, for a rare movie and dinner out. It seemed a little odd that they hadn't asked me to go along. Even though I wouldn't have gone—I'd been looking forward to working in the darkroom—not being asked made me feel like they were keeping something from me. Maybe it was just all the other secrets swirling around—maybe I was getting a little paranoid.

I'd just finished printing some pictures I'd taken weeks ago—four or five great ones of Raz in front of the trash squares at the dump and a couple of bikini shots that Harley wanted extra copies of. I hung Razzle's photos over the bathtub and Harley's near the wall—I didn't even want their *images* in close proximity. Somebody started banging on the door as I was cleaning up, but I didn't rush. I figured it was one of our guests with an urgent need for a new shower curtain or some other so-called emergency.

Razzle, soaking wet, was the last person I expected to see standing there when I opened that door.

"Can I . . . could I come in for a minute?" she asked.

"Jesus," I said, ushering her inside. "How long have you been out in this?"

"I rode my bike over." She stood on the tiny rug in front of the door, water dripping off her drenched sweatshirt and running down her bare legs into a pair of ragged sneakers.

"You rode all the way from Billie's in *this?*"

"I had to get out of there. It was awful." She was shivering so badly her voice shook too. "Billie's crying like crazy. I've never even *seen* her cry before. *Never.* And now she can't stop. She's been crying all day and I'm getting scared."

"Why's she crying? Wait a minute—you're freezing." I looked for something to put around her, to warm her up. Since I never showered in the cabin, the only towel around was one small dish towel, fairly useless in this situation. The closest thing at hand was the thin bedspread on my bed—it wasn't warm, but at least she could dry off on it a little. I draped it around her shoulders, and she huddled inside it.

"What happened? Why is Billie crying?" I took the dish towel and wiped the water off her face, blotted some of the wetness from her hair.

Razzle looked at me sadly. "Randolph died."

For just a minute I couldn't think who Randolph was. One of Billie's ex-husbands? A brother? The name was familiar . . . "Your *dog?* Randolph the *dog,* you mean?"

"Of course Randolph the dog. Do you know any other Randolphs?" She pulled the bedspread tighter. "He was her first dog, her oldest dog. I guess . . . I guess she really loved him."

She looked so small and pathetic and bedraggled standing there dripping on my rug. I'm embarrassed to admit it, but I really wanted to go get my camera and take a picture. Fortunately I had enough sense to know it would be a terribly rude and insensitive thing to do, even to your muse. Damn.

"You know what?" I said. "You have to get out of these clothes and dry off. Then tell me the whole story." She followed me into the bedroom and stood shivering while I looked through my drawers. She was lucky to wash up on the doorstep of somebody almost as skinny as she was.

I handed her a pair of jeans, a sweatshirt, and a pair of socks. "Is this enough? I can take your stuff down and put it in the dryer after you change." She nodded, barely moving. "Use the bedspread to dry off, or . . ." I looked around, opened another drawer, "just use some of my T-shirts. I'll put everything in the dryer."

She was still standing there in the middle of the room when I went out and shut the door. I wondered if she'd just stand there, if I'd have to go back in and help her. But after a minute I heard her moving around. It was weird to think of Razzle taking her clothes off in my bedroom. Not the same as imagining Harley taking *her* clothes off . . . which I had often imagined at length. No, it was mostly strange to think of Razzle being so . . . vulnerable.

Finally she came out and handed me a wad of wet cloth. I threw on a slicker and dashed down to the laundry shed to stick the stuff in the dryer, trying to pay no attention to the tiny white bra and underpants folded neatly inside her shorts. By the time I got back Raz was sitting on the couch, her legs drawn up under her, hugging herself.

"You still cold?"

She nodded. "Can you make tea or something?"

"Sure. I've got a bigger sweatshirt you can put on over that one too."

"Okay."

She was quieter than I'd ever seen her while I bustled around getting her more clothes and boiling water, and she was still all curled into herself when I brought her cup over and sat down next to her on the couch.

"So, now, tell me exactly what happened."

She took a deep breath. "Last night I noticed that Randolph was acting kind of funny. He didn't eat much dinner, and then he didn't want to go out and run with the other dogs, either. He was just lying under the table."

"That's unusual?"

"Oh, yeah. Randolph loved to be with the other dogs. He was very social. Anyway, I said something about it to Billie, but she was in a pissed-off mood, as usual lately, and she just said, 'He's an old dog. Ya expect him to get up and dance for ya?' You know how Billie gets real sarcastic sometimes."

I nodded. "Runs in the family, I guess." I was trying to lighten the mood, but Razzle overlooked it.

"So this morning when I woke up I heard Billie in the kitchen, sobbing. You've never heard anything like it, Kenyon. I never have anyway. It was terrible, like some wild animal caught in a trap or something. She was sitting on the floor with Randolph's head in her lap. Billie, who's always so strong, just *broken!*"

"He was dead already?"

"Must have died during the night. He was pretty old for a dog. Almost thirteen. But the worst part was that Billie kept saying it was all her fault. That if she'd listened to me and taken him to the vet last night he'd still be alive. Which probably isn't even true. She kept saying it over and over—I couldn't stand it." Raz put her head down into her hands. "It was like I didn't even know her anymore. Like she wasn't even Billie, just some sad old woman."

I put a hand on her arm. "She's just upset. She'll be okay. People get very close to animals."

"Yeah. Closer than they do to other *people,*" Razzle said,

anger suddenly thick in her voice. I could hear her own tears rising to the surface.

"It must have been a shock for Billie to wake up and find him dead like that," I said.

Raz looked at me for a minute, fury sweeping across her face, and then pain. "I loved him too!" she finally shouted at me. "I loved that old dog as much as she did!" And then she cried—big, howling, snotty tears that came from deep inside.

I pulled her close and let her cry on my shoulder. I could feel her shoulder blades shaking under my hands like little bird bones with each sob. I'd never even had a hamster, but I could imagine what it must feel like to lose a pet, especially a big goofy, forgiving mutt like Randolph. But I also knew that wasn't the only thing Razzle was crying about. She was crying about her whole screwy life.

I looked down at her hands lying across each other, palms up, like useless wings. There was Rusty's mole—Razzle's now—her hand-me-down mark of eccentricity . . . or maybe strength.

Finally she calmed down and got embarrassed. "God, I *never* cry," she said.

"Another thing you and Billie have in common."

"I guess so," she said, sniffling. "Did I get snot on your shirt?" She brushed at my pocket while simultaneously pulling herself away.

"No big deal," I said.

She nodded, wiping the sleeves of my sweatshirt across her face. "It *is* a big deal, though. Thanks, Kenyon. There's nobody else . . ." She stopped talking and bit her lip so she wouldn't cry again. I almost wished she would. I liked holding her little bones.

I knew she was uncomfortable about crying in front of me, though, so I tried to lighten the mood. "Hey, you know what?"

"What?" she said sullenly.

"Now Billie can get another dog! It won't be number thirteen—it won't be an unlucky dog!"

She gave me a lopsided smile. "Yeah, I guess Randolph was the unlucky dog, huh?"

I laughed and she did too, just a little. She held out her cup. "Get me some more tea before I send you back out in the rain to rescue my underwear."

I bowed to her wishes and pretended we had not just had a remarkable half hour.

I didn't see much of Harley or Razzle in the week before the show—Harley and her mother drove up to Boston for a few days to visit somebody or other, and Razzle was busy hiding out in the playhouse "finishing up my art project" for the Dump Art Show.

I'd called her on Monday to find out how Billie was, but she wasn't too eager to discuss it. All she'd say was that Billie was pretty much back to normal and they'd buried Randolph under some rosebushes. I think the whole episode really scared her—Billie's breakdown and then her own—and also the fact that I knew about both. She changed the subject to her project as soon as possible.

"I can't wait for you to see it. You know, I always wanted to make things, but I was afraid I couldn't make them look the way they do in my head. But then, when I saw your photographs, I thought: He's a kid and he's making things—why can't I? So, I just *did* it. I guess you were sort of my inspiration too."

"I'm glad," I said. She sounded so happy I couldn't bear to tell her I was cutting the *Angel of Mysteries* series in half—it had meant so much to her that I was using it for the show. And when she saw whose pictures were replacing hers . . . well, it wouldn't be a pretty scene.

Mrs. Thackery moved back into Shearwater for the last week of summer, just like she said she would. I felt a little shy for about two seconds, until she said, "Kenyon, do you think you could stop by my cottage this evening after I get things arranged and help me decide which pictures should go into the dump show? My friends back home know so little about art, and they're too darn polite to tell me the truth, anyway! I need a sharp, intelligent eye like yours."

I figured she was just being nice, but I was looking forward to seeing how she'd finished up the paintings she started earlier in the summer, so I went by to see her around midnight when I knew she'd be all set up. I brought two extra lamps from the storage shed.

"Oh, you remembered!" she said, lifting one of the lamps from my arms. "Thank you, Kenyon—I do need more light. But more than that I need your advice. I'm just standing here in the midst of everything, trying to make sense of it." She'd leaned canvases up on the kitchen counter, against the walls, along the back of the sofa—there must have been twenty paintings in all.

"Wow, you did all these this summer?" I asked.

"I had a very satisfying working season," she said. "I think it's because I got such a good start here in June." She sighed. "But now comes the hard part—picking what to show. Of course I can show some of them at our little gallery in Watkinton too, but it's in Truro that people really understand the work, so I always want to show my best work here."

She was quiet while I looked at the paintings, busying her-self plugging in the lamps, and then making us cups of tea. At first I was nervous, worried that she was counting on an amateur like me to help her make what seemed like an important decision, but by the time I got halfway around the room, I relaxed. The paintings were so beautiful, so full of color and light and life, it wasn't a question of making a wrong decision, just of which paintings would show best together.

By the time I got to the last paintings, I was shaking my head. "These are wonderful, Mrs. . . ."

"Stop! There's no Mrs. in *this* room!"

I smiled. "Sorry. I meant, Lydia."

"That's better. I let your parents call me Mrs. Thackery because they wouldn't be comfortable with it any other way. But you're an artist. Between artists there are no distinctions based on age. I can learn from you as well as you from me. If you call me Lydia, I'm your peer."

"Well, I don't know about that . . ."

"Absolutely true. Now continue. You were saying how wonderful my paintings are." She laughed. "No really, Ken, I don't want the whitewash—just tell me which you think are best."

I let my eyes circle the room again. "I really do like all of them. But since you can't put twenty paintings this size in the show . . ."

"Let's say three or four, at most," she said.

"Well then, you want them to complement each other."

"That's right. I knew you'd understand this."

"Well, you've got to put that Chelsea Clinton painting in,"

I said, pointing to the first one I'd seen her work on last June.

"Chelsea Clinton? That's a self-portrait!" she said.

"Oh, right," I said, laughing. "I dreamed it was Chelsea Clinton." I told her all about the dream I'd had after that first night I watched her paint, and she laughed until tears rolled out of her eyes. Then we got down to business and chose four paintings that looked good side by side, all of which sounded like the ocean at midnight.

twenty

I slept late the morning of the Dump Dance and Art Show. I'd finished up the bathroom the day before—no one seemed to notice it had taken me two weeks to paint the tiny space which was already half covered with tile—and my summer job was now officially complete. Of course the summer was almost officially complete too, the season winding down quickly. We'd keep a few of Baker's Birdhouses open on weekends through the fall, but I'd have to close up Mockingbird soon and move to my room in the big house.

In another week school would start. Although I'd decided to attend Provincetown High with Harley, Mom still hadn't gotten around to taking in my records from Hancock. I tried to imagine starting a new school, meeting a bunch of new people. It made me nervous to think about it, but having a great-looking girlfriend would definitely help.

Harley was picking me up around three and taking me to the dump so I could hang my pictures. All the artists were supposed to have their work hung before five o'clock in the big white tent that had been set up in back of the Swap Shop. It would then be locked until the "opening" around eight o'clock tonight.

I had a few hours to kill, and not much left in my own refrigerator, so I wandered up to Mom and Dad's. The car was gone so I figured Mom was out grocery shopping or something, but when I walked into the kitchen she was sitting at the table, the newspaper spread out in front of her, drinking coffee.

"Whoa! When was the last time I saw you sitting down in the middle of the morning?" I said.

"Good question," she said, folding the paper. "You must be hungry—that's about the only time I see you anymore." I don't think she meant to sound snappy, but she'd gotten so into the habit of it this summer, she could hardly say anything anymore without seeming angry.

"I can get it," I said. "All I want is a bagel and juice, anyway."

"I'll make you eggs, if you want," she said, without much enthusiasm.

"Nope. I'm fine. Did Dad go somewhere? I see the car's gone."

I was busy getting my breakfast together, and it took me a minute to realize she hadn't answered me. I turned around. "Mom?"

She sighed and patted the table. "Sit down a minute, Ken. We need to talk."

"What?" Fear suddenly shot through my body. "Is something wrong with Dad?"

"No, no, nothing like that."

I relaxed a little and sat down, but I was still worried—we hadn't *needed* to talk in ages. "What's going on?"

She sighed. "Dad drove up to Vermont this morning."

"Vermont? What for?"

"We've been talking to some people up there who have a bed-and-breakfast they're selling. We saw it listed in the paper and we called them . . ."

"Wait a minute. A bed and breakfast in Vermont? You can barely take care of this place much less another one."

A sad little smile curled one corner of her lip. "Ken, if we bought that place, we'd sell this one."

"What! We just *got* here! We just fixed it up!"

"I know. But the realtor says our improvements will make it much easier to sell. We won't take a loss."

"You've already talked to a realtor? When were you going to tell me?" I shot up from the table. My life, I realized, was totally in their control. I was like some pet that got moved from one place to another at their whim.

"We were going to wait until your father got back, but since you asked, I thought I should tell you now. Ken, I know it seems sudden to you, but this place is too much for us. The Vermont house would be more manageable. And besides, it hasn't worked out here the way we imagined it would. I don't think we're really Cape people."

"Well, *I'm* Cape people. I love it here!" I screamed.

She laughed gently. "Ken, three months ago you were bored silly, and you didn't like it one bit."

"I know, but I wasn't in love then!" I burst out, surprising even myself with the use of the L-word.

"In love! Since when? Not with that Razzle person!"

I hadn't meant to say anything at all, but now that it was coming out, I might as well tell her the whole thing. "Not Razzle. You don't even know what's going on with me anymore! I love Harley!"

Now it was Mom's turn to be flabbergasted. "*Harley?* Oh,

my God, Ken. She doesn't even wear any underwear! She's named after a *motorcycle!* You can't possibly be in love with someone like that!"

"Well, I am, and I'm not moving!" I screamed, knowing that when it came right down to it I had no alternative but to go with them wherever they dragged me. I picked my bagel from the toaster and walked out the door, no butter, no cream cheese, no jelly. No choice.

I decided not to say anything to Harley about moving. We hadn't actually bought the new place—maybe it wouldn't happen. Besides, I remembered how it had been when I announced I was leaving Boston. The few friends I had acted sad for about ten minutes and then began to ignore me, like I was already gone. Alex was a little better—he came over the day we left to say good-bye. But I could tell he was in a hurry to get going—we were over now—he had other things to do.

Anyway, I had the show to think about today. Harley picked me up at three, and I loaded her backseat with the photographs. It had been agonizing to decide which pictures to leave out of the *Angel of Mysteries* series. I'd ended up with five pictures of Harley and five of Razzle, plenty for my small amount of space, especially since the two groups didn't seem to have been taken by the same photographer. It was awful having to hang them so close together. The cutesy pictures of Harley looked even sillier next to the carefully composed shots of Razzle.

Harley didn't notice it, though. Actually I don't think she even looked at anything else except the pictures of herself—and she thought they were fabulous. Or maybe she just thought *she* was fabulous, but since I did too, I didn't argue with her. In order to get all the photographs in my space they had to be hung five over five, and, of course, Harley thought hers should go above Razzle's. When I saw them hanging there together I felt more than a little sick. What would people think—that I didn't know the difference between them? What would Lydia think? I knew what Razzle would think, and she'd be right.

There was a middle-aged guy setting up some large pottery jars while we were there, but most people seemed to have brought their work earlier. I saw Lydia's paintings from across the empty space, and they looked wonderful. Then walking around I saw one of Eddie Bacheldor's sculptures, too, although I didn't quite get it—a bunch of golf clubs welded into an arch over the top of a couple of demolished fenders.

"Let's go. I need time to get ready," Harley said.

"Just a second. What's that thing?" There was a sheet-covered mound about three feet high and three feet square sitting on a table along the back wall. As I got closer I could see the sign taped to the front of the sheet.

DO NOT LOOK AT THIS BEFORE THE SHOW!!—RAZZLE

I had to laugh. Her secret project had to be kept secret until the last possible moment for the greatest dramatic effect. That was Razzle. I wondered what on earth she'd made.

Harley grunted. "For God's sake, who does she think she is? What's the big deal, anyway?" She started to pick up the bottom of the sheet.

"Harley, don't!" I said, knocking the sheet out of her hand.

She looked at me in total surprise. "What? Am I gonna turn to dust if I look at her monstrosity before tonight?"

"She doesn't want anybody to see it yet. I think we should respect that."

She looked at me with as much disgust as if I were a dead rodent. "Respect? Gimme a break. You are so into obeying all the rules." She turned and trotted out of the tent, back to her car.

I ran after her. "Wait a minute."

"I'm leaving now," she announced. "If you want a ride home, get in. Otherwise, learn to drive." It was a particularly nasty comment, I thought, pointing out, as it did, that I was younger than she was, if only by a few months. We drove back to Mockingbird in silence.

Harley pulled the car up sharply in front of my cabin and jerked to a stop. "What is it that you *like* about her?" she asked me.

"What difference does it make?" I said, hoping to calm her down. "I just like her as a friend."

"But *why?*" she wanted to know. "She's *weird.*"

That was true, but then, Harley had said I was weird when we first met. "I don't mind the weirdness. I sort of like it. Of course, not in a *girlfriend,*" I assured her.

"That's the dumbest thing you've ever said." She wasn't pouting—she was just mad.

I gave up. "Well, if it is, I'm sorry. You still want to go with me tonight, don't you?" I put my hand on her arm and rubbed it softly, but she flicked me off like a fly.

"Of *course,*" she said, unconvincingly.

"What time?"

She sighed. "I'll pick you up at seven. I sure wish you could drive."

I slammed the car door a little more firmly than I probably should have, but I really wasn't enjoying the abuse. As the car roared off I thought, *you're lucky you're gorgeous.*

twenty-one

Harley looked amazing, and she was in a better mood, too. When I crawled into the front seat, she flung one black-stockinged leg across my knees to show me her shoes, little red straps that barely held her foot to the high, spindly heels.

"How can girls wear these things?" I said, trying not to seem as overwhelmed as I felt by the nearness of her glamorous limb.

"Girls can't; *women* can." She had on a ton of makeup, but it wasn't garish—it just made her eyes look enormous and her mouth look dark and wet. It occurred to me that at fifteen and three-quarters I was not quite ready to be dating a woman, even if she had just turned sixteen. And when she parked at the dump parking lot and got out I could see that all of the above merely hinted at the complete look. Her slinky black dress was low on top, high on the bottom, and showed every single body part inside it. If my mother had seen her, we'd be headed for Vermont tomorrow.

Most people were dressed up, but not like Harley. There were more Birkenstocks than high heels, and people wore long scarves, bright colors, and lots of funky jewelry. A crowd was already dancing to the music of Primo's Progress, as the band was now called, and a bonfire was burning wieners and marshmallows next to the recycling shed. A table next to the Swap Shop was lined with donated casseroles and soft drinks. You weren't supposed to bring liquor because the dance was open to all ages, but Harley assured me people brought it and kept it in their cars. In fact, she had a mayonnaise jar filled with gin under the front seat of the Volkswagen, she announced, from which she'd already had a few swigs.

"Before you picked me up?"

"Yeah."

"You drank before you drove?" What I really meant was: You drank before you drove *me?*

Harley rolled her eyes. "Would you grow up, Kenny? God, you are so . . . different."

"I thought that was what you liked about me."

She looked at me like she was trying to remember why on earth she'd ever said such a thing. "Well, at the moment it's getting on my nerves."

She slithered over to the food table, and I didn't really want to follow her, to tell you the truth, but I was hungry. Harley, of course, wasn't getting food, just a Diet Coke. I piled a paper plate with coleslaw, potato salad, and red beans while she wandered off into the crowd. Fine with me. We needed a little break.

There were a bunch of folding chairs and benches set up around the dancing area, so I took my plate over and sat down to watch. Young women swirled around with babies in their arms, twelve-year-old girls tried to swing dance, and old folks threw their arms in the air and shook their booty. There was a little bit of everything going on out there, but I guess that's what you'd expect at a dump dance. With all the old hippie garb they were wearing and the bonfire blazing in back of them, the dancers looked vaguely tribal. It reminded me of that Kevin Costner movie, only this one was Dances With Artists.

Of course we weren't out in the wilderness—we were at the dump. The recycling shed and the Swap Shop roofline were draped with Christmas lights—Razzle's work, no doubt—and the Dumpsters had discarded stuffed animals, some missing ears and tails, tied along the sides with clothesline. The white tent glowed like a temporary palace, a fantasy temple of art that would be gone by tomorrow. It was an incredible scene.

I recognized Lydia's bright pink scarf before I saw her face; Eddie was swinging her around in a kind of polka or something, and she looked like she was having a great time. She waved at me as they whirled past. Across the dance floor Ezra and Mimi were occupied with each other, their headlights locked and motors purring, apparently unaware that Primo had kicked the music into high gear. As I was watching them, Billie came up and interrupted their clinch—she was all excited about something and poor Ez was getting an earful, but I couldn't tell what it was about.

I was so involved with watching them, I didn't see Razzle approach.

"Did you know that if Barbie was life-size she'd be seven feet, two inches tall?" She plopped into the chair next to me, barefooted and dressed in dump chic, as always.

It was good to see her again. I'd been thinking about her a lot since that rainy day Randolph died. Thinking about what it would be like to be raised by a character like Billie who cared more about her dogs than her human relatives. In some ways Razzle's life, isolated on a Truro dune, had been just the opposite of mine growing up in a city apartment, but in other ways, more important ways, our lives were similar. For example, we were both afterthoughts.

"Hey!" I said. "I figured you were here somewhere. Did you do the decorations?"

"Course I did," she said. "How's the coleslaw?"

"It's good. Did you make that too?"

She nodded. "Took me all afternoon. I had to set up my project this morning."

"Yeah, I saw it in there, covered up. Can't wait for the unveiling."

"Me either. I hope you like it." Her usual manic energy had returned, and she bounced in the chair. "I can't wait to see your pictures either. Of course, I get a little credit for those too."

She was grinning like crazy, and I remembered again what my photography exhibit looked like, *The Angel of Mysteries* cut in half and stuck beneath the *Cosmopolitan* cover girl. How could I ever explain it to Razzle? She'd never forgive me. Suddenly I totally regretted letting Harley ruin my exhibit like that. Just so I could feel her boobs a few times? Was I nuts? Of course, if she really did come to Mockingbird tonight. . . .

"Your girlfriend's dancing with some scuzzbucket," Razzle reported.

Sure enough, Harley was pressed up against some guy with tattooed Paul Bunyan arms and a bad bedhead. "How old is that guy, anyway?" I said.

Razzle shrugged. "Twenty-five or six. Wouldn't be her oldest. Oops. Sorry. Forgot who I was talking to for a minute."

"She's got her good points," I said, although at the moment I'd forgotten what they were.

"Name one," Razzle said, of course.

I sighed. "Do we have to talk about Harley? You know we just argue . . ." Razzle was looking over my shoulder, and her eyes got wide. "What's wrong?"

"Let's dance." She jumped up, grabbed my hand, and pulled me into the middle of the moving swarm of dancers. She turned so that I was between her and the parking lot.

"Who are we avoiding?" I asked, craning my neck around to look.

"Rusty. Don't let her see you. She's crazy today. I don't want to be around her."

"Crazier than usual?"

"Yeah. She went to see Frank," she said. "Something's going on—I gotta stay out of her way."

"What do you think is going on?"

"I don't know, and I don't wanna know."

The band swung into a slower, jazzy tune, and a few couples headed for the bonfire, but most of them just moved closer together and kept grinding their hips. Harley and Mr. Bunyan certainly seemed to be enjoying their close contact. I grabbed Razzle's hand and pulled her close to me too, but she stumbled over my feet.

"Watch it!" she said, as if *I'd* stepped on *her.*

I guess I'd never actually slow-danced before. It didn't look that hard, but you had to coordinate your steps if you didn't want to trip each other, and neither of us was very good at it. On top of that, we couldn't turn around much because Razzle was still hiding from Rusty—she kept her face smashed against my shoulder. We must have looked ridiculous swaying back and forth in place, kicking each other's ankles.

"You never mentioned what a fabulous dancer you are," I mumbled.

"Oh, and you're John Travolta," she said. "Just dance me where I can't be seen."

"Tell you what—put your feet up on my sneakers."

She looked at me. "Like little kids do?"

"Yeah. You can't weigh much more than an eight-year-old anyway. Then we won't keep stepping on each other." So she did. With her bare feet up on my shoes and my arms around her waist, she was very close to me and stared right into my eyes in that unnerving way she has. I circled us around and through the pack, until we were back by the bonfire. It was fun, holding her like that. And dancing in the firelight was almost, I don't know, romantic, which I would never have imagined feeling in connection with Razzle. She looked oddly calm.

"I'm glad you moved to Truro, Kenyon."

"Me too, Raz." I felt really good for a minute, but then, suddenly, I had the feeling Razzle was going to do something weird. I don't know what—cry again maybe, or maybe even *kiss* me. She got a funny look and it scared me. I said the only thing I could think of to say, to diffuse things. "Did you know Marilyn Monroe had six toes on each foot?"

She looked surprised for just a second, then looked away and gave a short laugh. I was afraid I'd hurt her feelings, so I pulled her a little closer and she let me, her stubbly hair tickling my cheek.

It's possible we both had our eyes closed because we didn't see Rusty coming. By the time we did it was too late to make a getaway.

"There you are!" she said, grabbing Razzle's wrist. "I been lookin' for you."

"I'm busy. Leave me alone." She turned away from her mother, but Rusty didn't let go.

Just then Frank appeared too, looking sweaty and pissed off. It was great to see him again, but he was in no mood for pleasantries. He put a hand on Rusty's shoulder. "Let's get out of here before you make a fool of yourself in public," he said.

"Again," Raz added.

Rusty tried to shake him off. "You're the one who says I have to tell her the whole story. So lemme do it. That's what I came back for, anyway—to get him off my back once and for all so I can start living my life again. Ezra's already figured it out—once I tell her I'm leavin' this damn town and I'm never coming back."

Razzle put her hands over her ears and backed down off my feet, the better to escape, but Rusty was still hanging on to one wrist. "I don't want to hear anything you have to say," Razzle said. "Go away!"

"This is not the time or place for this," Frank said. "We'll do it tomorrow if you want to."

"I won't be here tomorrow. I'm doin' it *now!*" Rusty stomped her foot and glared at Frank.

Frank sighed and put one strong arm around Rusty's shoulders and another around Razzle's. "Well, not right here on the dance floor," he said as he muscled them toward the bonfire. "At least we can get out of earshot of every soul on the Outer Cape."

"Can I come too?" I called after them.

"Yes!" Razzle said. "I want Kenyon with me!" She seemed desperate, scared.

Frank motioned to me to come and I followed them to an unpopulated spot in back of the fire.

Frank began. "There are a few things we think you ought to know, Razzle . . ."

"*We?* I'll tell her—she's *my* kid."

"Just barely," Frank shot back.

"This is about my father, isn't it?" Razzle said, her voice shaky, her teeth chattery.

"Yes, it is," Frank said, calming himself down. "Your father was a good friend of mine."

"He was a better friend of *mine,*" Rusty said with a mean laugh.

"I doubt that."

"Listen, Frank, you don't . . ."

Razzle looked back and forth from one to the other. "Just tell me if you're going to! Who is he? What's his name? Where did he go?"

"His name was Angelo Flores," Frank said. "He was a fisherman on my dad's boat. We both were."

"*Angelo Flores,*" Razzle repeated, feeling the name in her mouth. "He lived . . . in Provincetown?"

"Born and raised," Frank said.

"Born, raised, and died," Rusty said, taking it one terrible step farther. I could see the gravestone now, the one in the Provincetown cemetery that Frank tried to visit every day. *Angelo Flores.*

"He's . . . dead?" Razzle looked so fragile, standing there with that roaring fire behind her. Did she really have to know all this? Rusty had let go of her wrist, so I took her hand.

"That's enough for now, huh? Let's get out of here," I said.

"No!" Razzle said, clenching her teeth and shaking me off.

"I might as well know it all. I *should* know it. I need to know it." She looked at her mother. "Tell me all the bad news. How did he die?"

Rusty looked more sober now, for some reason. She chewed her lip for a minute and then started in. "He was my boyfriend in high school. We were in *love*." She made a face as if to show how silly they'd been. "I got pregnant. With Ezra. Angelo wanted to get married, but I was only seventeen, for Chrissakes. I said, no thanks. I wanted to get out of this stifling place and see something in my lifetime. I didn't want to be *married*. Do I look like some fisherman's wife?"

"That upset Angelo," Frank said, breaking in. "He was raised in a Catholic family. That wasn't the way you did things . . ."

"I'm telling it," Rusty said.

"You have to tell the whole story. You can't make him sound . . . crazy!"

Rusty sighed. "No, he wasn't crazy. Except for being in love with me. *That* was crazy. Anyway, I had the baby, and we stayed up at Billie's house—you can imagine how pleasant that was. I still saw Angelo. He was a big good-looking guy. Ez looks like him. So do you, now I think of it. Anyway, a year or so goes by—I get pregnant *again*. Stupid, just stupid. I know Angelo is really gonna bust a gut this time."

God! Rusty is standing there telling us how stupid it was for her to get pregnant, as if we don't all know that child was Razzle, this person right here, the one shaking so much I'm afraid she's going to fly apart. I put my arm around her to help hold her together.

"*Now we gotta get married,* Angelo says. *I wanna be a father to my children,* he says. Like I have no say in the matter."

"He should have had as much say as you did," Frank said, chewing the words up and spitting them out. "He actually *wanted* to be a parent."

They just stared at each other for a long minute, and I began to hope they'd decide to end the story there. I didn't want to know the rest. I didn't want Razzle to know the rest. It couldn't be good.

Finally Frank said, "Finish it."

She sighed. "So, I'm a terrible person," she said, as if she didn't really believe it, but then before the next words came out, tears slid down her cheeks. "I lied to him. I told him an awful lie."

"What?" Razzle said in a whisper.

Rusty let herself cry a little, then continued. "I told him the baby wasn't his. I said I'd been sleeping with some guy up in Orleans too, and it was his baby. You were." She shook her head. "There was no other guy. I just said that because he made me so mad, the way he insisted I had to marry him. If I'd known . . ." She cried again, but kept on talking. "By the next day I felt so bad about saying it . . . I was gonna tell him the truth, even though it meant he'd start up with that marriage stuff again . . . but I was gonna tell him the truth—I really was . . . only when I got there . . . when I got to his place . . ." She looked up at Frank, who had his arms crossed tightly over his chest. "I can't tell her this, Frank. I can't." She bent over and sobbed.

Frank looked up at the sky and sighed deeply, then reached out and laid a hand on Razzle's shoulder. She was standing quietly now, almost numb, I thought. Frank finished the story. "Rusty was too late. When she got to Angelo's place, he was dead. He'd hanged himself."

Razzle's eyes went wild, and she pulled away from Frank and me. Rusty sobbed louder, and people all around us were looking.

"I know this is a lot for you to take in, but I want you to know that Angelo was a wonderful person," Frank said, crying now too. "Too emotional, maybe, too dramatic. But he loved Rusty, and he couldn't stand the idea of her being with somebody else. He was young and passionate, but he wasn't crazy."

I could hardly take it all in myself. Hanged himself! That was the kind of thing you read about in books, or saw on a TV movie. Or maybe you read a newspaper article about some kid doing it, but it was never somebody you knew. Of course I didn't know Angelo Flores, but I felt like I did, through knowing Frank and Razzle. And even though I didn't know what he looked like, I had an image of Rusty walking into one of those little white P-town houses and finding his body. That would just about make anybody crazy.

Right about then Billie and Ezra came running up, Mimi trailing behind.

"You told her, didn't you?" Billie said to Rusty. "Right out here. Just because it was convenient for you."

"It had to be done," Rusty said, sounding hollow. "Maybe now his ghost will stop following me around. I've spent half my life running away from Angelo Flores, and I'm tired of it."

Razzle looked at Billie. "Did you know? Did you always know?"

Billie squared her jaw and faced her granddaughter, one hand awkwardly patting Razzle on the shoulder. Her eyes looked kind of watery to me for somebody who never cried. "Of course I knew. Everybody knew at the time. But when

Rusty left—and then Frank, too—people stopped talking about it. I figured if you didn't go into Provincetown much, stayed up at my place, you wouldn't hear about it until you were old enough to take it. Maybe I shoulda told you, but I didn't think it oughta be up to me to explain things." She shot an evil look at Rusty, who just stared back.

Razzle looked at Ez. "You knew too?"

"Not for long, Raz. I just found out this summer, working in P-town. I didn't know how to tell you." He put his arms around her and she fell against him. "We're okay. We're not like Rusty or Billie," he whispered to her. "We're like each other."

"Or maybe, like *him,*" Razzle said.

twenty-two

Right about then Eddie started yelling that the art show was open and we should all go into the tent. Of all the terrible timing—I was ready to shoot myself. How could I have let Razzle down like this? Now she'd think she couldn't trust me, either. Fortunately, our group was still reeling from the latest news, so we didn't rush right over.

Rusty was the first to get herself in gear. "So, I'm leaving. I'll get my stuff at the house and then I'm outa here." Ezra and Razzle stared at her as if they'd never seen her before. "Look, I'm *sorry,* okay? I can't undo it! I would if I could, but I can't!"

"Just go if you're goin'," Billie said. "Don't drag it out."

"Where you headed?" Raz asked quietly.

Rusty shrugged. "Not sure. Maybe Pennsylvania. I got a friend there."

"Send me a postcard?" Razzle asked.

Rusty gave her a crooked smile. "Sure, kid. I'll keep in touch."

That was all anybody had to say to her, so she turned around and walked to the parking lot, got in her crappy old car, and left.

Frank let out a big sigh. "Razzle, Ezra, anytime you want

to talk to me about Angelo, well, I'll be waiting. But I think enough has been said tonight. I'm gonna go see the art show. Peter's probably over there already. Anybody coming with me?" I knew he was just trying to make things feel more normal again, help everybody get going on their regular lives again. He didn't know what was hanging in that white tent. I wished I didn't know either.

Billie said art didn't interest her, but I think she just wanted to get away from the scene of the crime. She hiked over to the casseroles.

By the time the rest of us went inside the art show, it was too crowded to see anything but the exhibit right in front of you. I figured I could buy a few more minutes if I headed straight for Razzle's exhibit.

"Hey, come on, Raz," I said. "I've been waiting to see this for months now. Unveil, please!"

She'd been so excited about making this thing, and now her moment was almost spoiled. Almost. When she reached up to grab the top of the sheet, there was still a little of the usual sparkle in her eyes. She was proud of herself.

One good snap, and the sheet was off. Sitting on the table in front of us were two figures, one male, one female, and underneath them the title of the work: *Mom and Dad*. They were remarkable.

Mom had a barrel for a stomach, but the front of the barrel was cut away and a mirror glued into the hole so that when you looked at the sculpture you saw yourself peering out from inside it. Two cream-filled chocolate candies, like the kind you get in a Valentine's box, served as breasts. The head was a toaster with two old paperback books popped out of the toast slots: *I'm O.K., You're O.K.,* and *How to Talk to Your*

Troubled Teenager. On the front of the toaster Raz had glued beer bottle caps for eyes, pink feathers for eyebrows, and a crazily skewed rubber band for a mouth. Mom's arms were wire hangers and her legs cut-off rag mops. A naked rubber baby doll was hooked on one of the wire hangers, right between the eyes.

Dad's body was a big old television set with two antennas sticking up in the air. At the ends of the antennas were post-cards, one of a car dealership in Illinois and the other of girls in bikinis on a beach in California. The old golf clubs she'd kept from the set Eddie took formed criss-crossed arms and legs. On the front of the TV screen Raz had pasted cutouts of cartoon characters: Superman, Archie, the Joker, and a bunch of evil-looking weird ones I didn't recognize.

Both the creatures were encrusted with tiny pieces of junk from Razzle's collection: shells, sea glass, buttons, ribbons, jewelry, broken dishes, plastic flowers, little toys, all the stuff I'd seen waiting in buckets in her room last June. This was what she'd been saving them for.

"These are wonderful, Raz," I said. "I'm knocked out by them."

"Really?" It seemed like she couldn't let herself be too happy about anything right then.

Ezra put his arm around her again. "Wow. I didn't know you could do stuff like this." Mimi was enthusiastic too, and Frank just kept swallowing hard, as though he didn't dare open his mouth. Finally he bent down and kissed her cheek.

"I think you're my hero," he said.

Raz sighed, but she looked awfully confused. "Okay, we've been here long enough. Let's see something else. Oh, let's go see my *other* exhibit. Kenyon's pictures."

My stomach flopped over. At first Razzle didn't see where they'd been hung—I guess it hadn't occurred to her that Harley would be shrieking and giggling in front of them. When she did figure it out, her shoulders slumped.

"Oh, dammit, *she's* over there. I should have known." She kept moving in that direction, though, and I couldn't think of any way to stop her.

Harley was flirting like crazy with the male member of a couple who'd stopped to look at the photographs.

"These are from my *portfolio*," she said, staring into the guy's eyes. "I was going for a sort of romantic look."

Oh, let me fall through a crack in the earth, I prayed. I hung back as our little party stopped in front of the pictures and took in my betrayal.

"There's the photographer," Harley admitted to the couple, "and the other . . . subject." They smiled politely and slipped away as Harley's attention was transferred to us.

Harley and I were both looking at Razzle, waiting for her reaction. Harley wasn't disappointed.

Razzle turned to look at me, but I couldn't stand to see the hurt in her face—I looked away. "I know I should have told you. What happened was . . ."

Her voice was low. "I know exactly what happened. I just never expected it from you, Kenyon. Not from you."

"Hey!" Harley said. "He can show pictures of anybody he wants!" She slipped her arm around my waist, the first time she'd done that, I realized, in a week or more.

"Raz, listen. I'm sorry. I . . ."

"You don't have to apologize to her, Ken," Harley said.

"No, *Ken,* you don't have to apologize to me. You don't even have to speak to me again. Ever." And Razzle was gone.

She dodged through the crowd like a quarterback and disappeared out the door. I made a move to go after her, but Harley still had a hold on me.

Ezra gave me a funny look, part anger, part pity. "I know her hiding places. I'll find her," he said, and he and Mimi took off too.

As soon as they were all gone, Harley let go of me like I was on fire.

The rest of the evening was a foggy nightmare. Frank was upset, although he didn't say much. I almost wished he would. I wished *somebody* would get mad at me and just say it: *Kenyon, you're a real jerk.* I was, at least, saying it to myself.

Both Peter and Lydia talked to me about the pictures. Not surprisingly, they both liked the *Angel of Mysteries* shots, but wondered why I'd included Harley's photographs. They weren't "up to the quality of the others." I couldn't admit that I'd included them because Harley had promised to sleep with me—they'd think even worse of me than they already did. So I just agreed with them and said now that I saw them hanging together I realized the difference in quality. Frank snorted. I think Lydia figured it out too, but she didn't let on. All she said to me was, "Be true to the work, Kenyon." What she should have said was, "Be true to your friends."

I wandered around the tent staring at the other work, but hardly seeing it. At some point I saw Mimi and ran over to find out what had happened.

"I came back to let you know we found Razzle in the playhouse. She's with Ez now, but she's really upset, Kenyon. This has been a terrible night for her."

"I know that, and I feel awful about it. I want to go talk to her . . ."

Mimi shook her head. "I don't think you should right now. She really doesn't want to see you. She doesn't want to see anybody."

"Where is she?"

"She's going to stay with Ez and me for a few days. In P-town. Let her be, Kenyon."

I nodded. "Okay. As long as she's all right."

Mimi gave a sour laugh. "She's anything but all right. But seeing you isn't going to help matters."

I don't think I ever felt worse. I felt so bad that the final blow, delivered by Harley, of course, didn't even sting that much. Or maybe I just wasn't as crazy about her as I thought I was. I was sitting out by the dwindling bonfire, just to get away from everybody, when she came swinging over.

"Listen, can you get a ride with Frank or somebody?" she said.

"A ride? I thought we were going back to Mockingbird tonight?"

She screwed up her face. "Kenny, come on. I mean, we're pretty over, don't you think?"

"*Over?* I put your photographs up! You said that tonight we could . . ." What was I arguing about anyway? Did I really think this night was suddenly going to turn into a sexual fantasy even though so far it had been nothing but a horror story? "When did you decide we were over?" I asked her, just for the record.

She gave a dramatic sigh. "God, Ken, these things don't last forever. What did you think? We were gonna get *married* or something?"

"No, but . . ."

"It's not that I'm not grateful, Ken—I am. You know, I took my portfolio to a modeling agency in Boston last week. They were very impressed." She laid a hand lightly on my arm. "I think they could tell a real photographer had taken the pictures."

I was struggling to keep up. "You took my photographs to a modeling agency?"

She nodded. "Yeah. Didn't I tell you? They pretty much told me they'll call me for jobs now. Jobs in Boston! So thanks for taking the pictures."

"You didn't tell me you planned to use them to enhance your *modeling* career." My blood pressure was definitely rising. "Was that the idea from the beginning?"

She pulled back. "No! That's a lousy thing to say. It's just that once I saw how good the pictures were, I figured there was no reason to waste them."

"You could have at least asked me."

Now her face clouded over too. "Look, Kenyon, you're a nice guy, but I *told* you I'll do whatever I have to to get myself out of here. I'm not spending the rest of my life going to *dump* parties!" She swung around and strode off toward the parking lot, where the tattooed Bunyan guy was standing by her car, waiting.

From around the other side of the bonfire Primo appeared, two hotdogs speared on a pointy stick. He put a hand on my shoulder as he walked past. "Call me sometime, man. We'll talk."

"Need a ride home?" I was still standing by the fire when Frank came up an hour later.

"I don't know what I need," I said.

"Well, let's start with a ride home," Frank suggested.

I followed him to his truck. "Isn't Peter coming?"

"He's got his own car here. Remember, I started this evening by chasing Rusty all over town."

Oh, yes, the first disaster of the evening. I tried to imagine how bad Razzle must feel if I felt this rotten. I didn't want to know.

Even though I was silent on the ride to Mockingbird, when we got there I suddenly didn't want to be alone. "Could you come in for a few minutes?" I asked him.

He thought it over. "I guess. Just don't expect me to be a shoulder to cry on this evening. I feel bad for you, Ken, but some of this you brought on yourself. It's Razzle who's really suffering."

"I know that. I just want to talk a little."

He followed me inside and plopped down on the couch. "Make me some coffee. I'll be less grouchy if I don't have a headache."

I got the machine going and sat in the chair across from Frank. "I know I really screwed up. What should I do? What *can* I do?"

"About Razzle, you mean? Or Harley?"

"Harley is history. She took my photos to a modeling agency, and now my usefulness to her is over. She dumped me at the dump."

Frank winced. "Sorry, pal."

"That's all she ever wanted from me. That, and maybe to screw Razzle around a little bit more."

"I'm sure she liked you too. You're a likable guy."

"Whatever. You're not surprised, are you?"

"Well, let's just say she didn't look like a keeper."

I nodded. "I guess I'm just dumb about girls. She was my first girlfriend. And she was so beautiful . . ." It was funny—already when I thought of Harley, she didn't seem so beautiful anymore. I hadn't forgotten what it felt like to kiss her, to run my hands up under her shirt, but now I also remembered that phony pout, how angry she got when things didn't go her way. It wouldn't be that hard to get over her.

"So, you learned a few things—that's not so bad," Frank said. "Maybe you even learned not to put *beautiful* on the top of the list. Next time you won't be so dumb."

"If there is a next time."

Frank laughed. "Get back on the horse, kiddo. Don't let one little fall spook you."

I tried to laugh. "I guess."

Frank got up to pour the coffee into mugs. "So what are you planning to do about Razzle?"

I leaned back in the chair. "What *can* I do? She doesn't even want to talk to me."

He handed me the e.e. cummings cup. "Not tonight she doesn't. She will, sooner or later. You remember what I told you before?"

"That she likes me?"

"Crazy about you."

"Not anymore."

"Oh, she's hurt—that's for sure. But the biggest hurt tonight was the shock Rusty gave her. That's a deep one, and it'll take her a while to work through it. What you did was a nasty slap, but she'll get over it. If you work at it."

"*Should* I work at it?"

He laughed. "Well, that one's up to you, Kenyon. I can't

pick your girlfriends for you. But Raz is the genuine article—I think you know that."

"Yeah. Was her dad like that too? Kind of crazy but really . . . great."

Frank's face softened. "Yeah, he was. Really great." He got lost for minute, thinking about Angelo Flores, I guess. Then he said, "Finding Razzle is the best thing that's happened to me since I got back here. She's like him all over again. I'm gonna watch out for that girl, Ken. I'm gonna make sure her life gets better."

twenty-three

Frank stayed until about one o'clock. He told me all about his childhood, about growing up with his best friend, Angelo. How they'd been inseparable from the time they were little kids, and how Angelo was the only person who didn't flip out on him when Frank announced he was gay. And about how, when Angelo killed himself two years later, Frank had been the one Rusty called, and how it had been the worst day of his life.

When he left, I walked him out to his truck. "You should tell Razzle all that stuff about Angelo," I said.

"I will, eventually. When she's ready to hear it."

"Thanks for telling me," I said.

"Thanks for listening, kiddo. Take it easy. Don't beat yourself up too much."

He'd barely pulled away when my mother's voice cut through the darkness behind me. "We need to talk, Kenyon."

I jumped about six feet. "Mom! Jeez, you scared me. What are you doing here? It's late."

"It certainly is. Could we go inside, please? I don't feel like broadcasting our problems to the whole place."

What problems? Did she know about Harley? Or Razzle? Impossible. Nobody could have told her because she didn't *know* anybody. I followed her into Mockingbird, and she closed the door tightly after me.

"I don't get it . . ." I began, but she interrupted me.

"No, *I'm* the one who doesn't get it. First you hang around with that arrogant dump girl, then you announce you're in love with a sneaky, half-naked chambermaid, and now I catch you ushering a thirty-five-year-old gay man out of your cabin at one o'clock in the morning!"

"What?" She was so off the mark I had to laugh.

"Oh, you think it's amusing? I'm just grateful your father stayed over in Vermont and isn't here having one of his sleepless nights. I can't imagine what *he'd* say."

"Say about *what?* You're jumping to a ridiculous conclusion. Frank gave me a ride home from the Dump Dance, and I asked him to come in for coffee. That's all."

"You *asked* him to come in? At this hour?"

"It was eleven o'clock!"

"And now it's one o'clock! This man is *gay*, Kenyon. Do you know what that means?"

Did she think I was eight years old? "Of course I do. It means he sleeps with other gay men. In particular, his lover, Peter. But not with fifteen-year-old straight kids."

She shook her head and leaned back against the wall. "You're so innocent. I admit it's partly my fault. I gave in when you arranged with your father to be allowed to stay in this cabin by yourself for the summer. I knew you were too young for so much responsibility, but you've always been a mature boy, and it never occurred to me that you'd make all these strange friends here."

I'd had about all the crap I could take for one night. "It never occurred to you that I'd make *any* friends, did it? And that would have been just fine with you because then you wouldn't have to spend one minute worrying about me. I'd just keep on being your good, lonesome kid, behaving myself like a perfectly boring dork you'd never lose a moment's sleep over. Isn't that right?"

She looked shocked. "Of course not. You've never been boring or lonesome . . ."

"How would you know?"

She opened her mouth and then closed it again. When she finally spoke, it was quietly. "I came here to tell you something important, Ken, not to argue with you."

"So tell me. I'm tired. I want to go to bed." I turned my back to her, picked up the sponge from the sink, and began to wash out the coffee cups.

"I'm tired too," she said. "But I wanted you to know as soon as possible that Dad bought the place in Vermont. The bed-and-breakfast. I wanted you to have a chance to get used to the idea."

I dropped the sponge back into the sink. "Already? He bought it *already?*"

"He liked what he saw. He called me, and I thought it sounded perfect too. We offered a price and it was accepted."

I turned to face her. "Which means?"

"Well, fortunately the house there is already empty, so we can close up the cottages here next week and put this place on the market right away. I want to be up in Vermont by September fifth when school starts. No sense in you missing the beginning of the school year."

Immediately tears started rolling down my cheeks. I hated acting like such a kid, but I couldn't help it. "And I have no say about this? I just have to go along even though I love it here? Even though I have friends here? Even though this is the best place I've ever lived?"

"Ken . . ." She reached out to touch my arm, but I jumped back.

"You can forget about me getting used to the idea because I never will!" I yelled at her. "I hate you for this. I really hate you!"

Her lips gathered up in a tight little circle. "This is the kind of behavior that makes me certain we've made the right decision in getting you out of here, away from these . . . low-class types of people."

It was such an awful thing for her to say that it shut me up, at least temporarily. It even dried up the tears. When had my mother become so frightened, so bigoted? Had she always been like this and I just never noticed?

"*Gay* people, *low-class* people, *strange* people—you can't tolerate anybody who's the least bit different from you," I said.

She let out a disgusted sigh. "I'm not making judgments against them . . ."

"Yes, you are!"

"I just feel more comfortable around the sort of people I'm used to, and these aren't them!" she said. "I would think you'd feel the same way."

The truth was suddenly clear to me. "But these *are* the people I feel comfortable around. And I just found them!"

She opened the door. "I'm sorry you feel that way, Ken. But we're leaving in a week. You'll just have to take my word that it's for the best." She went out and closed the door behind her with a brisk slam.

No, I won't take your word for it, I thought. *I'll never take your word for anything again.*

* * *

That week was horrible. Razzle refused to talk to me when I called Ezra's place, and then, when she moved back to Billie's, she hung up on me herself. Primo stopped by to tell me that Harley had gotten some modeling jobs through the agency in Boston—he wanted to have a bitchfest with me, but I wasn't quite ready. Harley was part of everything I was leaving behind, so I couldn't really hate her yet.

One of the hardest things was saying good-bye to Lydia Thackery.

"I'm sorry to hear your folks will be selling the place. You've done such a good job fixing it up," she said. "And where will I find someone else who'll stay up talking with me about art until the wee hours of the morning?"

"I really don't want to go to Vermont," I told her.

"Oh, Vermont is lovely too."

"No place is like here, though."

Lydia laughed her kind laugh. "Oh, my dear, you've gotten Cape Cod sand in your shoes, haven't you?"

I nodded. "And I can smell it now too."

"Smell what?"

"The aroma you talked about the first night I met you. The ocean and the sand and the air and the whole Cape Cod thing." I took a deep breath. "How can I leave here now?"

Lydia put her arm around my back, which was as far up as she could reach. "Kenyon, you'll only be gone for a while. I think it gets in your blood as well as your shoes. Folks like us all come back eventually."

I helped her pack her canvases into her car and stood on the highway waving until she rounded the corner half a mile away and was gone.

★ ★ ★

The day before we were due to leave, there were a few odds and ends to be cleaned up. And trash to be hauled to the dump. I loaded it into the back of the truck, all but one broken lamp and a wrapped package that I held on my lap. Dad drove me over. I guess Mom knew what I'd do when we got there, and she couldn't stand to witness it.

On the way over, Dad tried a little conversation. "I guess you're not too happy to be leaving."

"Nope." Why should I keep trying to explain myself? They didn't really care anyway.

"Your mother was so unhappy here. Ever since the beginning . . ."

I'd heard this rationale already. I had no comment.

"And with my back . . . the work load at the new place will be a lot lighter for both of us." He gave an uneasy laugh. "After all, we *are* supposed to be retired."

Then just retire, already—retire from parenthood, too, and leave me alone. I thought it, but I'd never really say something like that to Dad. He's already such a sad guy.

"I'm sorry we're switching you around like this though. I feel very bad about it."

The good boy bobbed to the surface. "It's okay, Dad. I'll live."

He patted my shoulder and pulled into the dump parking lot.

Dad stayed in the truck—he'd finally admitted that he only set himself back when he overdid it with something like heaving trash bags over his head. When I'd gotten rid of everything else I went back and got the lamp and the package from the front seat.

"I'll be back in a minute, okay?"

"Sure, Ken. Take your time. I'll pull the truck over in the shade." Clearly, my mother had prepped him about this trip. And his guilty conscience was working to my advantage. I had to admit I still loved the guy, even though I didn't always like him anymore. Maybe one of these days I'd be ready to say the same about Mom. But not yet.

When I walked in Razzle was sitting on the floor sponging off a couple of plastic Big Wheels. She turned around when she heard me come in, squinted her eyes at me, and then turned back to her work.

"I brought you something."

Silence.

I set the lamp on the floor next to her. "I wouldn't dare throw a lamp away when you can probably fix it."

Silence.

"Raz, I'm leaving tomorrow. Won't you at least talk to me? I'm really sorry!"

Silence. She scrubbed those plastic tires like she was planning to drive the thing in a parade.

"I brought you something else, too." I dropped the package in her lap. She stopped scrubbing and stared at it as if it might explode.

"What is it?" she said. Speaking!

"Well, open it."

She sat looking at it for a minute, trying, I guess, to decide whether or not to obey my directions. Finally she ripped the tissue paper off in one motion.

I'd framed my favorite photo from the *Angel of Mysteries* series, the one where she was leaning against Loon, her leg forming a V against the cabin wall, the line of cabins receding into the distance behind her. The one in which she seemed quiet. It was the photograph in which I knew her best—the one I thought of as the *lonesome* photograph, though I'd never tell her that.

Razzle stared at it a long time, then laid it on the floor next to her. "Thanks," she said.

"Will you talk to me now?"

"You think that's all it takes? One picture and I'm not mad at you anymore?"

"No. But I'm leaving tomorrow . . ."

She whirled around and threw the soggy sponge at me. "Then leave! Just get out of here!"

I brushed at the wet spot on my shirt. "It's not my fault I'm leaving! I don't want to go!"

"Why not? Harley dumped you, didn't she? You might as well get going."

She meant that to hurt me, and it did. But not because of the actual dumping by Harley—it hurt me that Razzle *wanted* to hurt me. "Come on, Raz. Stop it. I'm really sorry about everything. You know I am. I should never have put her pictures in the show—*they* were terrible, and *she* was terrible, and I'm sorry!"

For a minute she didn't say anything, but then she spoke again. "You were wrong."

"I *know* I was . . ."

"Not about that. About the secrets. I don't like knowing them. Don't like it at all."

I wished this could be like the day Randolph died, when she let me hold her and cried all over my shirt. But her face was tight as a newly plastered wall today—there was not going to be any leakage. "I know, but someday you might be

glad you know. Angelo Flores was a good guy. You sho.
talk to Frank about him."

"Maybe." She stared at my shoes. "I guess you'll never come back."

"Yes, I will. I definitely will. I plan to."

She snickered. "Plans don't always work out."

"These will," I promised.

She turned back to the riding toy. "Well, come and see me when you get back then."

"I will."

"Bye."

"Bye." There didn't seem to be anything else to say, so I started to leave. But then I thought of something else. "Hey, did you know that Elvis Presley didn't have a belly button?"

She spun around again. "Did you just make that up?"

I smiled, and then, for just a second, so did she.

ty-four

Vermont in December. The plows have been working all night, but the streets are still icy. They almost never call school in this place—everybody's always bragging about how they aren't going to let a few feet of snow keep them off the roads. Fortunately this is Saturday; I don't have to go out, and not many people are coming in either. Our rooms are all filled for the holidays, but now, two weeks before, we're half empty. Everybody must be at the mall. A lot of our renters are cross-country skiers, but we're too far south for the big ski business. This is just a little bed-and-breakfast in a small college town. Mom and Dad are pleased.

Their moods improved almost as soon as we got here, and so did Dad's back. Last week he stuck that back mat out in the garage behind a bunch of boxes that never got unpacked from the Cape. There's not nearly as much work to do at this place with only four bedrooms to rent out, and Mom actually seems to enjoy talking to the visitors as she serves up their strawberry waffles in the morning. I guess they're "her kind of people."

I have a different relationship with my parents now. I'm not their good little boy; they don't expect me to be. I don't help out much with the bed-and-breakfast work; they don't ask me to. They don't treat me like a baby anymore; I don't allow them to.

As soon as we got here, I told them I had to have a bedroom with its own bathroom so I could set up my darkroom. I'd decided this point was nonnegotiable—after all, they'd just ripped me away from the place I loved. They could get more money for a room with its own bathroom, but they gave in to my demand without an argument. I guess they felt guilty even though they acted like we'd all just barely escaped from a sandy purgatory.

One night Mom came into my room and asked to see the pictures I'd shown at the dump show. "We were so caught up in moving at the time, I forgot to look at them," she said. A lousy excuse since she hadn't taken any interest before that, either. I guess standing up for myself has made me visible to them, too.

I handed her the photos of Razzle, the ones I was proud of. "Goodness, you make her look so interesting," she said.

"She *is* interesting."

"Well, I suspect the credit goes to your pictures. These are very good, Ken. I'm so glad we've moved someplace where you can have a darkroom year-round, aren't you?"

If she expected me to shower her with gratitude, she was disappointed. I know she's trying to make it up to me about the move, but she won't be able to. It's not so much that I'm still mad at my parents—it's just that I don't look at them the same way I used to, as all-powerful, but benevolent, dictators. I've found my own power.

I don't hate the town as much as I thought I would, either. Being the new kid in a school system where everybody else has known each other for a decade makes me sort of a big deal. I got my driver's license, and there's a group of kids I've started to hang around with—one of the guys even reminds me a little bit of Primo.

But there's nobody here like Razzle.

As the months passed, I thought about her more instead of less. I wrote her a letter, but she didn't answer it. Maybe I said too much about all the new things I was doing, as though I'd forgotten about our summer in Truro. I imagined her hanging around at Frank and Peter's place. Going up to the cemetery. I wondered if it was too cold to use the playhouse now, if Billie had gotten another dog. It killed me not to know.

Then a few weeks ago I got a phone call from Peter. He was getting ready for his first spring shows, and he wanted to know if I was interested in showing the *Angel of Mysteries* series for two weeks in May.

"Sure I am," I told him. "But I don't get out of school until June. Any chance I could do it then?"

He thought a minute. "I guess I could rearrange things a little bit—for my young star. Have you got anything else to show? A second series? In June you could have a little more space."

"I do! I've got a series called *The Muse*. It's Razzle at the dump."

"Sounds good. As long as it isn't that glamourpuss. We'll take your Razzle pictures anytime."

So we set it up. I have to get them all framed, of course, but I work at the local photo shop now so I've got a salary *and* a discount on supplies. I can hardly believe it. I'm going back to Cape Cod in June. Somehow. I haven't actually told Mom and Dad about it yet, but I'm sixteen, I can drive, and I'm going.

So I fired off a postcard to Razzle. There was an Escher print on the picture side.

> *I shall return on June 8th for two weeks. Peter is showing* Angel of Mysteries *and our second collaboration:* The Muse. *You see, I kept my promise.*
>
> *Kenyon*

I thought for sure she'd send me back a postcard with something slightly nasty scribbled on it. But day after day, nothing came in the mail, which made me miss her even more than before. I wondered if all her anger—at Rusty and Billie and even Angelo—had gotten dumped onto me. Not that I didn't deserve a large part of it.

So I've been thinking that I want to write her a real letter, not some newsworthy thing about school or my new job. I got out the pictures I took of her last summer and spread them out on the floor so I could look at them all together. It was kind of scary seeing them again. I felt very nervous, as if I was going into an important test and wasn't sure I'd studied enough.

The thing is, Razzle looks right through the camera lens, like it's not even there. At least it seems that way to me. Who she is is no mystery to me anymore—it's right there in her eyes, which seem to see inside me. I want to be that honest with her, too—I'm just not sure how to do it.

So I decided to start at the beginning. I've got a legal pad—it could be a long letter—and I've started to write:

> *Looking back, I'd have to say my life was one long snooze until the day I met Razzle Penney at the Truro dump.*